DIARY OF A (FAT) JACK RUSSELL: AGED 11 AND ¾

By Rachael Alonzo

Chapter One: Weight Loss

Diary,

Wednesday

I have apparently got udders!! I've looked this up and it means I resemble a cow, a goddam COW! This can't be right as I am a dog, a Jack Russell, of sorts.

To be honest, I think, I was what is known as the runt of the litter, as I am a little on the stumpy side, in fact, I think I have dwarfism. Seriously, I have short legs, yes I know our breed is known for being small, but mine are like stumps. And I am not your typical energetic type, I am old, cantankerous and I like to live my life sedately OK, and I need to lose some weight, as I am a little on the chubby side, in fact a lot on the chubby side.

Oh and I use obscenities sometimes, only when annoyed (which is a lot of the time HA), and my all-time hero is Robert De Niro, and I sometimes pretend I am in one of his movies, like my alltime fave, Goodfellas.

But I have a big heart and massive paws (they are big for me), and I just love my Mum and Dad, they take special care of me and for a while now I have been sleeping in their bed so HA.

Anyway people, today is the day, I am attempting to get fit and lose these so-called goddam udders and so I am on a mission.

I shall come back later to report …

Well I'm back people, but briefly … I've managed a run, ha ha that's not technically true! it was more of a waddle, imagine a baby rhino trundling along after his Mum, you get the picture!

I have been given this biscuit crap, which I've got to be honest sticks to the roof of my mouth… I would sooner eat the stuffing out of my KK, short for Kenny Koala stuffed toy, a Christmas present I had one year. I always get a new toy, but shall tell you that tale later on, but for now needs must, and if I am to attempt to lose these udders, I suppose I had better eat this cardboard shit, and get back to being all DAWGIE.

Stats for the day

Treats eaten: 0

Birds stared at: 6 (they come in the garden all the time!!)

Pigeons barked at: 2 (these bastards land on the fence purposely to annoy me)

I'm off now people, as it's my morning nap. I have lots of these…

Thursday

Jesus H Christ what ungodly hour is this, 6.10 a.m.!! I am not getting out of this warm cosy bed, just because you have to get up Mum, doesn't mean I have to… but seeing as I am awake, what's for breakfast…

Oh yeah for one brief moment I forgot I was on a health kick...this sucks, I have saliva dripping onto my paws dreaming of bacon and sausage, mmmmm…

Snap out of it Rupert, oh yeah that's my name people, Rupert as in Rupert the freaking bear (what a camp bastard he was, all chequered trousers and a scarf!)… I mean I do kind of look a bit like a teddy bear, my face is proportionately the same, and it's tan in colour, the rest of me is white, however I think I'm more of a Fozzie bear! Cheeky, naughty and obnoxious.

Now, let me just scoot around a bit in the big bed, and I shall descend the stairs, and see what awaits… FLOP, oh that was just me getting off the bed and the sound of my udders hitting the floor, ha ha.

Well I've just spent the last 10 minutes staring at a bastard pigeon (whilst waiting for my dry crappy stuff), he has had the audacity to sit on MY fence and do this cooing thing and then he fluffs his feathers out, seriously mate you're not fooling anybody, YOU ARE a rodent with wings. If I had the energy I would jump up that fence and bite your feathery ass… OMG, he is shitting now and it's running all down the fence, you dirty bastard, I need to bark, ward him off, Mum will not be happy he's done that, ha ha, in your face, winged rat! My barking scared him off, I think that deserves a little treat; I shall go and see what slim pickings are on offer.

NIL, no treats were on offer people, as Mum said NO, until I have lost some of my udderage! PAH the cheek of the broad! This seriously sucks.

Well, I've attempted some sit-ups… in fact they were not exactly sit-ups, with my udderage it's more I roll over and then attempt to roll back... I look like a furry potbellied pig...this is no joke anymore, and yes I know folks I only have myself to blame, but when you love food, you love food.

I'm feeling a snooze coming on (I told you I was sedate!) so bye for now…

Dear Diary it's like Saturday

WTF… That has to be the longest snooze ever, I've lost a day and half, but the bonus is, people, it's Saturday and that means Mum and Dad are home ALL day! Whoop, whoop, I'm doing my happy dancing, running round continuously on one spot, oh that has made me dizzy, or has it, could it be because I am being STARVED TO DEATH!!! Gimme food.

I've had my walk and I tried to run a little bit faster today, the udderage was swinging low. I even spotted next door's cat, Ginger Bastard. Once, he had the barefaced cheek to stand his ground and hiss at me, that is until Mum extended my lead a little and I waddled up to him.

Who's the pussy now...in fact it was me because that bastard swiped me with his claw...my face, my face, nobody touches the face, I shall embark on that tale a little later, anyway for now:

BREAKFAST … more dry crunchy stuff...I can't talk right now...imagine crackers, dry, stuffed in your mouth...you get the picture

Stats…

Treats: 0

Birds stared at: 9 (it's sunny and they are all hanging out in the bird bath)

Pigeon bastards barked at: 1

Apparently, people, we are going to visit Nanny (she resembles a hamster) and Granddad (he looks like a potato). He really does...he has no fur at all!!

This day will be a challenge for me as they love, love, love, to give me treats, and as you know I'm on a campaign, but one won't hurt, right…

God dammit people"!! WTF, it's all gone pear shaped, fuck it... I had only been at Nanny's house 10 minutes when she whipped out the most mouth-watering divine-smelling treat I had ever smelt (my sense of smell is astronomical)… It was a peanut butter crunchy bone-shaped (it's amazing how they get them in that shape) biscuit. I tell you folks I scooped that bad boy up in my mouth and I was in heaven … 2 hours 15 minutes later this is the score:

Treats: 5 (yes you read that right!!) the shame …

Birds stared at: 0 (I just couldn't be bothered)

Pigeon bastards barked at: 0 (as above)

I was in peanut butter heaven and now I'm going for a snooze fest - all those carbs have zonked me right out…

Bye for now.

Hello again Diary

Sunday

I can't eat that many treats in the future!! I had an unfortunate situation and Mum and Dad are not happy, in fact they said I farted all night in bed, and now this morning their bedroom smells like a shit storm!!

Well I can't help farting, it's what I do, and anyway if you hold your farts in they travel up your spine and into your brain and then your head explodes… I got told this once by a German Shepherd…

Well folks I've successfully managed to lose zero weight - it's been 4 whole days and nothing, nada, zilch, so I don't know if it's even worth continuing, but apparently I've got to. Mum says I'm beginning to resemble a footstool… a goddam footstool … I don't think they realise I do have self-esteem you know…

Treats today: 0

Birds stared at: 10 (pecking muppets are all just sitting on the fence) Pigeon bastards barked at: 2 (dirty bastards are cooing at each other)

I'm off for a nap - it is Sunday after all…

OMG...I've been woken from my slumber by the most amazing tantalising smell...I'm pretty sure it's roast beef… I've followed the smell to the kitchen, and yes it's beef… BEEF…

How is this not torture? I'm sure there's a number I can call for this cruelty, isn't it run by what's his name, Paul something or other, I can see his face, he's on that TV show For the Love of Mutts! and he helps abandoned cruelly-treated dawgies, that's me.

You can't say I've got to cut back and then go and cook a freaking roast beef dinner FFS …

I'm going to shit in their shoes… on second thought, last time I did that I was about 4 or 5 and I got told I was a disgrace and a disappointment! I can still remember the guilt and the hurt look in my Mum's eyes… She has this stare, and seriously it frightens the bejesus out of me, so perhaps not…

Moving on: Beef, Beef, Beeeef… come to poppa… Ooo people I think I can hear carving… yes definitely carving… ooooo that's the sound of my bowl on the work top… oooooo I am going to investigate! Back in a mo…

I'M BACK

Oh god oh god oh god I am delirious from what I could see (bear in mind it's not much, seeing as how I am so low to the ground) but my bowl is on the work top and I swear there's beef in it… Please Jesus I promise to never chase squirrels again in the park if there's beef in my bowl…

I have to go, I'm being called folks...pray for me

Ha... I've had all my prayers answered and have just eaten the most amazing, moist, delicious mouth-watering beef you ever did taste! My Mum is awesome.

I cannot believe I was allowed this, but apparently it's ok in small quantities and my soulful big brown eyes did the trick… I hypnotised the crap out of her… oops sorry I meant I looked longingly at my Mum and she caved HA

I'm off for my fourth nap, yes that's right NAP NUMBER 4. Get over yourselves…

Diary today is:

Monday

Again what's with the early starts? Can't a dog just get a lie in!

Eaten the crunchy dry stuff (that's the end of the beef)!

Walked to the farmer's field, spotted Ginger Bastard on the way, pretended I was tough so raised my hackles a bit… and then guess what Diary… you are not going to believe it, we bumped into Douglas the Highland Terrier! He's got serious issues… every time he sees me it's the same, bark, bark, bark, bark. I'm sure he's a bit of a dummy or as we say now mentally challenged… I say the same thing each time: "It's me, Rupert"… But no it's like Groundhog Day!!

Nap time

Oh before I go, my stats…

Treats: 1 (I was a good boy) Birds stared at: hundreds (all in the farmers field. He won't be happy HA)

Pigeon bastards barked at: far too many to count on my paws - I'm not Einstein!

Something is off - I can smell it… The special blanket is out and I've been woken from my slumber… Ooh we're going on a journey… outside in the big thing with wheels…

Well folks, I'm not sure I want to talk about it …I feel too traumatised… I feel as though I've been abused…

We had to go to the vet's (the vet and I don't get along, I have to be muzzled). I thought it was a visit to the park, we sometimes go there, but NO - they made me get on these scales on the floor, everyone could see the number except me! There was gasps and then awwwws, but not good awwws or cute ones… There was a smug-looking sleek cat in a basket, she hissed and meowed at me, the shame was horrific. I am obese, people, freaking obese, how has this happened?

But that's not the worst… We had to go in a private room. I thought, my god they are going to perform experiments on me! especially when I was hauled onto this metal table.

I then had to endure the muzzle being put on me, and I swear to god I could hear tittering… I was like, do I amuse you, bastards? Anyway I think I look like Hannibal Lecter in it, anyone for a Chianti?

So there I am on the metal table, muzzled up, and Mum has me in a neck hold… I thought, what am I, a wrestler? piss off, and then that's when it happened - an object was inserted into my rectum! No warning, no "good boy", no "this won't hurt", it was just shoved right up there! And not for seconds NO, it had to be held in for 2 minutes to get my temperature.

It has to be the most disturbing, shameful thing that's ever happened to me… thank god folks my temperature was normal… not sure how my arsehole is feeling right now…

I have to go for a lie down folks… I feel violated…

Diary Yesterday was a bad day…

Tuesday

I had to stay in bed all evening. I wasn't able to show my face. I never want to discuss this again people...Capiche?

Well this diet malarkey is goddam useless. I am hungry all the time. I stare at my Mum and Dad's food when they are eating and I have a new technique for gaining their attention.

I adopt this soulful look, but then I've added a jump and a little whiny noise, and I do this move that makes it look like I am treading grapes with my front paws… So far it's not worked, but hey otherwise I'm going to waste away and die and who's going to notice…

On my walk this morning we passed this long flappy-eared mutt, his belly was lower than mine and he looked a bit dopey. I think he's called Bassett or something like that… anyway he looks just like his owner, ha ha ha, and they have the same walk… I wonder if he thinks the same of me and my Mum… she's small and stumpy like me, and yeah in fact has some serious fur going on, especially on her top lip, it tickles me when she kisses me HA HA…

Well I think as I am hungry, in fact starving, and all I can think about is food, I will go and have a little nap, as I am not going to get any treats today… Bastards!

So people, I shall report back after my snooze… sssshh sleeping

I'm back folks, it was only a short snooze fest, but I woke to the sound of such a commotion outside that I had to go and investigate. There is a situation! Magpies are lined up on next door's roof, there's at least 4 of them that I can see… I hate, hate, hate these squawking thieving bastards even more than pigeons, at least they don't hijack nests and kill innocent babies… These black and white bastards are the devil's creation.

I need to get out there, people! I shall be back…

OMG! I bolted out that back door faster than greased lightning, my udders were swinging, I was smokin', baby! I did my best impression of a lion, fearless and striking (the reality, folks, is I looked more like a fat capybara) but they didn't know that, did they? I chased them bastards right out of the garden! I can't have them unsettling my birds and their babies… I mean

I'd have nothing to stare at all day… they will think twice before coming back to this patch.

All that growling and woofing has made my belly rumble… I need food, I need subsistence and I need it now! Back in a mo.

Right I got to the kitchen, and trust me it's far for me due to my stumpy legs… Anyway I stood there all big brown eyes,

soulful, and I did my utmost to telepathically transmit my thoughts to Mum: Fooood, biscuits… I thought she would be pleased I chased the magpies away but NO, no, no, no - you know what she did?

Patted me on the head (I've said repeatedly NOT the face, you muppets) and said good boy Rupert, nasty magpies.

That's it, nothing, no biscuit, nil nada zilch, well she can piss off now if she thinks I'm going to chase them black and white bastards away again. She can do it herself.

Time for the compulsory nap, methinks…

Tonight I have mostly been lying down with my eyes closed… I mean there are no treats, no birds to stare at (it's dark out), no shows on TV that interest me… We have been watching Game of Thrones, I love this show, it's the only programme that piques my interest, oh that and Sir David Attenborough. I like to bark at the TV and Mum and
Dad think I am really clever! I can hear them say, "Oh look he can see the animals, he thinks they are in the lounge", daft eejits, I know they are NOT! I am not a dummy like Douglas FFS, anyway tonight it's positively boring.

Mum and Dad invited Nanny (hamster face) and Granddad (potato) round and they were playing some card game, gin was involved but don't know if this was the game or a drink…

Perhaps it was drink as Mum is now lying down with her eyes closed!! Weird, she is making some strange sounds… I think she has a dragon living inside of her, Holy Christ on a bike, someone come and save me!

I'm thinking of starting a Twitter account but can't decide on a name… I'll get back to you people once I've decided.

Chapter Two - Tweeters and My Patch

Hey Diary

Thursday

Bloody hell folks, I've slept for 10 hours straight… and I've missed a day, I couldn't be bothered yesterday at all. However, I've woken up with gusto and a Twitterati name - wait for it

- @Tubbyclown! What do you think? No? Well I did have a backup name - @Udderking!!

Get it? Udders… king of… oh piss off.

Anyway I heard Mum talking to Granddad (the potato) last night about how he finds it difficult to walk and exercise because of Arthur’s ritus or something like that… I'm looking it up

Well I think I've got that for sure, this Arthur’s ritus, definitely (what's weird is my granddad is named Arthur, maybe it's named after him), but anyway, that's me done for any exercise… can't put pressure on my delicate joints.

So people I have to rest, so off for a nap. Wake me if you hear rumblings in the kitchen…

I shall get back to you on the Twitter malarkey.

Treats eaten: 3 (don't judge me)

Birds stared at: 7 (I think they are scared after the magpie episode)

Pigeon bastards: 0... (They must be scared too bunch of pussies)

Bye for now.

Friday

Hey peeps it's Friday and you know what that means… Dad does shopping! Ooooo yeaaah… Food foooood fooood, however I'm still being given this dry stick-to-the-roof-of-your-mouth crap, so might go on a hunger strike! They better start giving me something tasty soon, or I'm going to die… Whoever said "it's a dog's life" was a twat!

You try being this low to the ground and all you get to see are feet… rugs… floor… more feet… And all that neck craning is not fun.

Anyway Dad will be back soon, and he better have some decent treats… Oooh maybe he has cheese! I love, love, love cheese, in fact the only time I get cheese is when there are tablets hidden in it. They think I don't know that's what they're doing… I DO KNOW, I AM NOT STUPID. I accept the tablets because that's how much I love cheese!

Oh you want to know what the tablets are for… Well people I have allergies… I am a sensitive little soul, every year in the summer the pollen gets me… I have itchy paws, an itchy face and itchy ears, and MAN it drives me insane, because I have to rub my face round and round on the rug and then I end up with carpet burns, I chew my paws until they are red and GOD my ears…

So I have to take anti-whatsits or something to stop the itching, and I have to be bathed with a special medicated shampoo in the bath… I pretend I don't like it but really I do, it's heaven, the feel of the cool water on my paws, oooh lovely! Mum even sometimes washes my dingle dangle (which doesn’t really work now, but that’s another story).

So I am a very delicate dog… It's the white fur, it’s apparently more prone to sensitivity, and as I am mostly white with the odd patch of tan around my lovely teddy face, it's a given that I get to suffer in the summer, so what with being a stumpy bastard and my allergies and compulsive behaviour I am a proper stunted runt!!

Well I can hear Dad, he's back from shopping, so I am going… I have to do my customary dance-round-his-legs routine and wait to see what offerings there are… See you in a mo.

Whoop whoop… yeah baby… guess what I've got? The biggest dental stick EVER… It's ok to have because it's for my teeth, so before you say anything… FUCK off!

Mm mm nom nom nom mmmmmmnomnom nom nom mmmmmmm

Oooh I'm loving this!

Bye peeps!

Oh treats: 1 (this big stick)

Birds stared at: 8 (they are getting brave again)

Pigeon bastards barked at: 3(on next door's roof, twat bastards)

Diary it's Saturday or FATURDAY… Ha ha…

People, I've done it! I've joined Twitter (or Twatter as I heard Dad call it when Mum said she joined!! Rude…)

So I've gone with @tubbyfootstool!! Because I am likened to a footstool, especially as Mum took a photo of her resting her feet on me and thought it was fucking hilarious… me not so much.

So I've already had 2 people follow me - TWO! That's awesome! They are a fat cat, so we have that in common, and a sweary cat, we also have something in common, so freaking great!

I shall now update you people with my daily tweets, and I've also decided to quit my diet… yes that's right, you heard, don't JUDGE (I'm too old and long in tooth for this crap)!

So off for an evening snooze

Treats: 4 (making up for all the ones I've missed)

Birds stared at: 9 (they are less stressed now)

Pigeon bastards barked at: 0 (they've got the message, methinks)

Sunday

It's a beautiful day folks, I'm up and happy, happy, happy! I've had 3 likes and another follow on Twitter… the likes were to my jokes, as you know I'm very funny… Do you want to hear them?

Penguin walks into a bar and says, "Have you seen my brother?"

Barman says, "What's he look like?" Oh god I'm rolling… ha, ha, ha…

Next one: are you ready, do you think you can handle this much comedy?

Man in a pub with a drunk giraffe lying on the floor… Barman says, "You can't leave that lying there like that"… Man says, "It's not a lion! It's a giraffe!"… boom, boom…

Oh I do amuse myself! Anyway the new follower is some pet rescue place, but that's good, I might need them in the future if Mum and Dad ever try and put me on some ridiculous starvation diet thing again. I mean, how would they like to eat dry brown crap…?!

So it's Sunday and it's supposed to be a relaxing day, however Dad looks like he's getting ready for some kind of sporting action!! He has on these ridiculous shorts, I can't stop laughing… and he's carrying some funny-shaped things, look like giant fly-swatters to me… but who knows??

I shall report back in a mo, off to sniff out some more clues…

I've found out people, I overhead Mum say, "well, have fun at badminton!!" (whatever that is), and she added, "don't try and do too much!!!" Sounds like he could have this Arthur's ritus thing then, if she's saying that he needs to be careful…

Well as Dad's away folks, I can have Mum all to myself… awwwww bliss! I shall go now as I feel a snuggly wuggly time coming on, no judging ok? In fact just fuck off.

I'm back after 2 hours of snuggles… I got in real close to Mum on the settee, yes I was allowed up, come on, if I am allowed on the bed, I must be allowed on the settee, right? Anyway I rested my head on her lap, and OH GOD heaven… I think I might've farted though at one point, as I heard Mum swear - something like "oh pissing hell Rupert… you smelly-arsed pig" - but I was so zonked out and happy I didn't care…

Anyway there's a situation and I think it's serious! Dad's back, but he looks a very funny colour, like glowing red in his face, and I don't know if it's raining out, but he's wet!!

Mum's shouting "Jesus H. Christ on a bike, go and have a lie down"… I'm going to investigate further…

Call an ambulance, call the police, call someone people! DO it! I think Dad's dead, he's just lying there on the bed… Oh wait, wait, he's breathing. Phew, I think he just overdid it at this badminton… but I've looked it up and it seems a genteel sport, so maybe my Dad's a pussy!!

I seriously hope not though, as I REALLY hate cats, especially that ginger bastard!

I've got to go people, I need to lie with my Dad until his face stops being so red. It could be a while…

I'm back, drama over, Dad's fine, he is back to looking his normal self (he looks a potato but with hair!), and I've been out in the garden, just mooching about really. I like to bury things and I have a special patch, I call it my serial killer patch, it's where I bury things I've stolen. So far in there is a sock, a deflated ball and Monkey Boy (a stuffed monkey but with some of the stuffing ripped out by MOI!).

I seriously need to add to my collection though, hence the mooching about… Ooo wait a mo peeps, I've just thought of something. I'll be back in a second…

I knew it, I just bloody knew it… For ages I've been looking for Froggy (a stuffed toy with no eyes, yes I chewed them out ok!). I thought he was lost… BUT NO! As I have an astronomical sense of smell (did I tell you my sense of smell is like 10 thousand times better than humans'?), I sniffed him out and he was IN THE BIN! The goddam bin… How dare they put Froggy No Eyes in the bin? He's my favourite.

So I whined and barked and danced on one spot at that bin until Mum caved and retrieved him out of there… poor Froggy No Eyes. I am so happy folks, so I'm off now. He can be added to my collection in my patch… I'm going to bury Froggy No Eyes good and proper.

Bye for now people. Dog sleeping… DO NOT DISTURB.

Hi Diary it's Monday… That came round quick…

Wake up, get up get up get up… HA I don't have to get up though, I can have a duvet day, Mum is home all day and so we are planning another snuggly wuggly day without Dad!

Oh bollocks! Pissing hell, Nanny (Hammy) has turned up. What's she doing here? She eats all our food… She better have brought treats if she intends on staying, ruined my day she has, ruined.

Oh wait… wait for it, she’s reaching into her bag…
I can smell beef and cheese, OMG this is awesome, I’ve gone delirious, I am actually in some kind of orgasmic smell heaven right now! Back soon…

You have no idea people about the taste explosion I have just experienced! It was a mouth-watering sensation, my Nanny Hammy is the best, the treat she brought was a rolled crunchy beef biscuit with cheese in the middle, and I got not only one but two of them!

I wagged my thumb-sized tail (yes that’s stumpy too!) and I actually squeaked with delight, I was that happy.

I have decided she can stay, it's not ruined my day after all.

Oooo I am being called people, methinks we might be going out… WE ARE, my lead is rattling, I can hear it. Got to go, will report back soon…

I'm back, and what an amazing bastard blimey day… we went to the park, and I caused a right riot with them duck bastards. Nanny and Mum took some bread for them, but I got in there first HA, you should've seen them, right bunch of dramatic quacking bastards all shouting at me at the same time.

I said chill boys I can't understand a word you're on about, quacking quack quacking at me, it's just some bread.

This is why people, apparently I am now confined to this extendable lead thing, because, off it, I am a bit of a lunatic (albeit a sedate fat one), but all the same I now have to be controlled… That in itself is freaking hilarious, I am a JACK RUSSELL (like I say a fat one) but still a law unto myself…

Anyway Nanny (Hammy) is going now, so I have to say goodbye…

Oh stats

Treats: 2 (ones from Nanny -delicious)

Birds stared at: well if you count the duck bastards, 15!

Pigeon bastards: 6 (they just had to get in amongst the ducks, didn't they!!)

Tuesday

Hi Folks

I forgot yesterday to check my Twitter, all that fun at the park, anyway I now have 10 followers, can you believe it… I heard Mum moaning to Dad saying I have more followers than her!! Well I do have a more loveable face HA.

Anyway the followers are a varied assortment of weird and wonderful people, and some dogs.

I have also had several likes to a picture I put on of myself in the garden mooching, they must like to see my face… like I say, it's cute!

I must be careful though, as I feel this tweeting malarkey could take over my life! Yes people I have a life, it consists of sleeping, eating, farting,
bird watching (wing and beak type) and barking at random objects and crisp packets (I thought it was a rat!).

Talking of rodents, we had a mouse come into the garden last week, and as I have excellent eyesight (along with my excellent sense of smell)(seriously I'm like the bionic dog), I saw that little squeaking vagrant come scurrying across the patio, and boy did I kick up a Ninja-style fuss, I was like a fat kung fu killer.

Mum came running in to see what all the commotion was about and I reckon she must have spotted it too, as I heard her shout the F word… Apparently you do not want rodents to get in your house, it would be the end of the world!! (I think she was exaggerating! again!)

Anyway I was still leaping 3 feet into the air (maybe now I'm the one who's exaggerating!) and I was barking for all I was worth, until finally

Mum opened the door. I bolted out onto the patio as fast as my little stumps could carry me, and I went sniffing with such gusto in the undergrowth that I came out looking like I had eaten a pack of liquorice HA.

However, squeaky mouse had obviously got wind of me and scurried off, good job otherwise that stinking vagrant would've been begging for his little rodent life and then I could've added him to my serial killer patch and to my collection.

Talking of my collection, you know how I buried Froggy No Eyes, well I also found an old sponge out of the shed. The door was left open yesterday, I sneaked right in there and grabbed it, that's now buried good and proper!

Well folks, I feel a snooze coming on…

Treats: 1 (#Mousegate distracted me)

Birds stared at: 8 (in and out of that bloody bird bath)

Pigeon bastards barked at: 4 (I am going to take you down!)

Thursday

I have had such a lovely snooze! It lasted 11 hours, wowzers, I think that's got to be a record for me, but maannn am I hungry! Food food glorious food, let's go and see what Mum has to offer.

Oooh she has bacon! I am seriously going to have to pull out the big guns if I want to taste any of that… back in a mo…

Did it work? I hear you say… DID IT BOLLOCKS! I must be losing my edge, I mean I sat all doe eyed, and I only tapped her once with my paw and I did a little squeaky whiny bark, but no nothing. I am seriously, really, well and truly going to die of starvation, then she will be sorry.

She will be all like crying and stuff and she will be the one doing the squeaking sounds (I've heard her when she cries, IT'S UGLY, Mum is an ugly crier!) and Dad will try and console her, but to no avail as I am her number one! HA, so she better take note. I shall give her one more chance.

Well I am being called FINALLY, it looks like it's my breakfast time… I hope it's good Diary I hope it's that stuff that has the sausage pieces in… Back in a mo.

Oh yeah, oh yeah, oh yeah, thank the baby Jesus, she has seen the light and I am now back on my favourite food! It's moist, it's crunchy, it's chewy and the taste is beef and chicken combined (how they do that I don't know) and it has small sausage pieces scattered in it, it's divine.

PEOPLE, if she EVER changes this again I will retaliate, I mean it! I like order and consistency, it's my compulsion you see, I must have everything the same, day in day out. Don't try and change my routine! IT'S THE LAW.

Oh I hear my lead, time for walkies… Yippee! Bye folks, see you in 5…

Chapter Three - Broads and Basil

I am back and OMG, you are never going to believe it, people… Yeah, yeah, we passed Douglas , it was the same old, same old, woof, woof, "it's me Douglas, fatso Rupert", woof woof… oh piss off, then we passed one of them dogs they used to do experiments on, a beagle I think, like as in Jeremy, goddammit I am so funny, anyway, NO this is even bigger news…

There's a new broad in town, and by broad I mean foxy lady. Whit woooooo, she is gorgeous, all golden brown fur, little stumpy legs like mine, a cute button nose, but dear god a mouth like a sewage farm… If we date she's going have to zip it a lot.

We passed each other and did the customary bottom sniff (thank god mine's recovered and smelt fresh!), we then circled each other and I doffed my cap (not literally ok, I don't own a cap, muppets!) but then she opened her mouth… Talk about get me some ear plugs… It was YAPPPY YAPP YAPPY YAPP high-pitched nonsense. I said "wow, broad, zip it" (I sometimes like to think I'm a character in a Robert De Niro film!).

What she came back with was even too extreme for you people, but it was along the lines of "Shut it, you F******G fatso c**t, where do you get off talking to a lady (lady HA!) like that, you stumpy clown?" I don't think I have ever heard such obscenities come out of a broad's mouth like that in my life.

Well that's it, I am smitten. I love a bit of rough… Oh you want to know what she is? Well I think she's a Pomerschizo or something like that!

I am going now people, for a snooze fest and maybe a dream or two! (An old boy like me has to have some pleasures!)

Friday

Yes Dad's gone shopping and he's back and yes I have my customary dental stick… nom nom nomm nommmmm…

Can't talk right now folks, I'm occupied… be back later…

Oooh ooh ooh, I have experienced a pleasure like no other, people, and it was such a surprise. Mum took me up into the bedroom, just me and her, and I thought, oh we are going for a sleep… BUT, it's not Night Night time (which is what Mum shouts when it's time to go upstairs for bedtime), strange… But then she produced this brush thingy (I'm gonna call him Basil!) and wowzers woof, woof, woof, she starting stroking my fur with it and brushing me, and I tell you I was in brush heaven.

Now you know I don't like my face being touched (I had a drama once, that's another story!) but she brushed my goatee under my chin (yes I have a beard! Ha, in your face, to those pussies who can't grow one!) and IT WAS BLISS. I mean seriously, it sent me dopey-eyed, I couldn't help it, so Basil and Mum and I have a new understanding, and brushy time is our special time, as long as afterwards I let her trim my nails. This last bit I really, really, really do not likey!

Last time she tried it, I swear to you people I almost lost my freaking paw… and then I had to be wrapped in a towel. Talk about looking like a twat, I mean I resembled E freaking T! Embarrassing.

So now we have brushy time and then I get my nails trimmed, as I am all relaxed and less likely to wriggle around. To be fair, it worked, so next time should be ok!!

Stats

Treats today: 2 (one glorious dental stick NOM! and 1 crunchy bone biscuit)

Birds stared at: 9 (in and out of that bloody bird bath, do they think it's a day spa?)

Pigeon Bastards barked at: 1 (I actually managed to jump up the fence at this winged rat… should've seen him, he crapped himself, literally! dirty bastard.)

Bye for now, off for a snooze fest, so ssssshhhhhh.

(I did warn you I'm sedate…)

Sunday

Hi folks I was totally zonked out yesterday and just couldn't find the energy to write, but I feel revitalised and have managed a walk this morning.

Checked my Twitter before I left and I have 25 followers now, it must be my dazzling good looks and sense of humour (did I tell you I'm funny?).

One comment even got more than 20 likes! I basically said just because I was old didn't mean I had Alzheimer's, I have what is known as some-timer's, sometimes I remember, sometimes I forget! Must be a lot of people out there who can relate. Hey come on people, this shit is funny!

I know my Granddad (potato) sometimes forgets, and when they visit, Nanny (Hammy) is always shouting at him, things like, "are you even on this planet?", and "you never F*****G listen to me!". That was the first time I heard Nanny swear. I have to admit that even though I use obscenities, this was shocking to me!

Anyway I also posted a great picture of myself in my serial killer patch with dirt and mud all over my face. I looked a right cutie, must also be a lot of crazies out there who like serial killers! HA

Well on the walk I did spot Pomerbitch (I can't remember the broad's name)… There's the movie compulsion again, but I steered clear. To be honest I can't cope with all that drama at my age.

Yes we passed Douglas, I mean seriously get counselling or something you arsehole, what is wrong with you? We also passed Ginger Bastard so it was an eventful morning. That pussy ginger muppet did swipe his paw as I walked past, and I said, "are you swiping your paw at me?" HA HA.

Dad is in his badminton outfit again (seriously you're killing me! what's with the shorts?) and so it's snuggly wuggly time with Mum, whoo hooo. Back later people, snooze fest coming on.

That was some snooze! I even snored, I went that deep. I dreamt of cheese and crunchy bones (nom, nom, nom), and when I woke up Mum must have guessed my dream, as she gave me a little baconflavoured bone (never had one of those before). It was ok but tasted a bit stale, I tried to convey this by spitting it out on the floor and just looking at it, but Mum (a bit of a gormo sometimes) thought it had just accidentally dropped out of my mouth.

I am not losing my faculties yet, broad! (Ha! De Niro again, sorry) so I picked it up and stuffed it right back in. I thought, ok might as well eat that baby, waste not want not, right?

HA HA HA HA Dad's back again, folks, and this time he doesn't quite look as beetroot red, but he's definitely off! Mum said, "why are you bothering if it's making you look like this when you get back?" I don't think he was happy with that comment, he's gone into the greenhouse (oh yeah we have a greenhouse - another story).

I am off now… I feel another little nap coming on. Be back later…

Pppffffttttt… What the hell was that? Strewth, that was NOT me… Freaking hell, the smell… I'm going, Jesus!

I am back, but only briefly. I have an upset stomach, I swear to god Mum has tried to poison me, I told you that bacon bone thing was rancid, it's given me the farts and MAAANNN they stink… phew wee…

Treats today: 1 (stale biscuit thing)

Birds stared at: 4(one of them was a robin, must be autumn)

Pigeon bastards barked at: 1 (he was a white and brown one, weird)

Monday

I couldn't come back yesterday at all folks, I was up all night, what came out of my backside was nothing like I have seen before. It was like ice cream, but not the nice flavoured stuff, NO this was toxic.

But I am glad to report I am now back to my normal cranky, sedate self. Now, what's for breakfast…

Oh Twitter went ballistic yesterday, I secretly tweeted a picture of my Dad asleep after his badminton and his sulk. You should've seen his face, mouth agape, saliva dripping, the works. Of course I photo shopped it and added a wig and a banana in his mouth, made him look like a right dick, he's gonna kill me if he finds out (I say if, he doesn't do social media, boring!). Anyway it had over 30 likes, so I now know what I need to do in the future, HA.

I wonder if Nanny (Hammy) is going to make an appearance again today and bring me some decent treats. I definitely do NOT want the ones from yesterday.

OOO I hear the door! I am going to run fast (HA) and see if it's my Nanny. Be back soon…

It wasn't Nanny, it was a delivery guy, some parcel for next door, again! What are we, like a UPS depot or something? I mean it seriously pisses me off (not that I have to answer the door, that would mean I'd have a job! lol). This neighbour must go online and order stuff every goddam night, and then he goes out to work the next day. F**K off.

Parcel after parcel, week in week out, his house must have so much crap in it. He has this hideouslooking statue thing of a plastic minger-looking meerkat outside his front door (seriously, it's ugly!). I bet he bought that online, or from one of those catalogues they put through your door, full of items like thermal tartan slippers (what's with the tartan? are all humans Scottish?). The only decent thing I saw in one of those catalogues was some little steps for dogs to help them into bed, now they were a freaking great idea… In fact I need those in my life. I'm going to try and see if I can get Mum to get some, back in a mo…

Well I have found the catalogue, tucked under a stack of newspapers. I have made a little mess, but so what, Mum can sort that (it's her job people, it's what she does ok), and I have left it open at the page by her side of the sofa. We shall see.

After all that mooching and sorting I need a little nap, and as Nanny Hamster isn't here I shall have a quick snooze, see ya later.

Mum has woken me up with such a racket! Oh Jesus H. Christ on a bike, what the hell is that? Oh, she's vacuuming! Now I don't ordinarily mind the vacuum, however, this bastard is new and it's like a big black snake… Aaarrrggghhh, it's after me, somebody help me, somebody call the police, or that show, I am going to die! I know, I'll bark at it, that's it, that will scare the bastard off.

NOOOOOOO, it's making it worse, Mum's laughing, why is she freaking laughing? "Does this amuse you?" "Is this funny to you?" "Am I like a clown?" Seriously, I need to take cover. I have to escape this room, I am going to the bedroom, the safe place. I shall let you know when it's stopped.

Well thank god that's over, that was horrific! Yeah ok maybe not to you, but I do not like new vacuum. Its name is Mr Harvey or something Muppetlike, well it can bugger off.

Treats today: 1 (I was too traumatised to whine for more)

Birds stared at: 2 (again, I had to run for cover)

Pigeon bastards barked at: 0 (good, they can piss off as well)

I didn't even check Twitter as I had to escape the black snake, but I shall report back later if there is any activity. In fact I am going to tweet my horror, that will surely get lots of likes.

I am going for another snooze, hopefully this one will be uninterrupted.

Tuesday

Ok, Ok, Ok I slept through and it's now Tuesday, big deal. I've been up hours again, Mum thinks it's great to get up with the larks, I think she needs counselling (like Douglas HA). Anyway, it means I have already been on a walk, and it's turned a bit nippy out there.

I could do with them tartan thermal slippers from the catalogue, ha ha ha ha. Talking of which, Mum spotted the advert for the little steps, and I heard her talking to Dad about them, well I don't think I am going to be getting them anytime soon folks.

I heard Dad say, "what the hell are they?" and "he doesn't need some little steps, the fat bastard just needs to lose some weight". I am seriously heartbroken people, I really thought Dad loved me as I was. I was so upset I had to have food and comfort from Mum, ha in your face Dad, you're not so slim yourself, chubby chubster (note to self, don't ever let Dad read this).

Anyway, back to my walk, we passed the usual crowd, Douglas, (the same old routine!), Ginger Bastard, Pomerbitch (that's her name now) and the beagle (I have decided to call him Ian… Ian Beagle - get it? No? oh piss off then, I am a comedy genius). So we are on our way back, then the most awesome thing occurred. There lying in the street was a football, a freaking football, oh my god, oh my god, oh my god, I just could not believe my eyes. I have this compulsion with footballs, so much so that I am NOT allowed them, in fact when I was much younger, fitter and not so fat, I had some serious footballing skills. (I swear to you I did.)

Anyway, before Mum spotted it, I waddled right over to it and tried desperately to grab it in my mouth, but: problem. Small mouth, big ball, not happening people. I needed to figure this out.

But then nooooooo, Mum spotted what was happening, and starting yanking me back in on this contraption she makes me wear (it's like bungee jumping, but without the fun!) and I am like really squeaking, and whining, and by now my eyes have glazed over, and I have taken on an all-new personality (this is what used to happen). I am in my ball zone, nothing or nobody is going to stop me from taking this bad boy home.

I tugged with all my strength on my bungee contraption and was back on that ball before she knew what had hit her, and then I managed to successfully puncture the cobblers out of that bad boy. The good news, VICTORY people, happy dance, happy squeaks… The bad news, zoned out, saliva in actual reams, dribbling out of my mouth, eyes the size of saucers, mud ALL over my face (I chased the ball round the dirt several times), Mum shouting quite forcefully leave it, leave it, LEAVE IT! She can BACK off, HA.

I am back home Diary, I had to leave it. Ok before you say anything, I am not a pussy, I did not give in easily. I trotted back with that bad boy in my mouth the rest of the way back home, with an awfully proud smug look on my face. However, when we got to the front door, somehow I think I got tricked, as Mum was like David freaking Blaine, she produced a mouth-watering, dental stick from out of thin air, and so I had no choice but to drop bad boy bally, and off I trotted inside to nom nom nom on my stick. (You know how much I love 'em). Anyway, some time later after dental stick heaven, I suddenly remembered bally, but when I went out into the hall to get him, he was GONE! NOOOOOOO.

This happened some years ok, I was tricked, but to be fair it was after I had smashed up the garden with a similar ball, that's why I am not allowed them anymore. It was a riot though, plant pots got smashed, shrubs were knocked sideways, plants kicked out, and the worst bit, the bird table was knocked over, yes knocked over, all by MOI. I was like a little whirling dervish, lots of shaking with it in my mouth, scooping it round and round with my nose and squeaks of pure delight, it was awesome folks. Oh those were the days! All this nostalgia has made me hungry and a bit sleepy, I can't decide what do to first, beg for another treat or sleep. Decisions, decisions…

Oh wait, I need to check Twitter first. Holy crap I now have 52 followers, that's freaking amazing, I am going to be famous soon, and then I can get them steps myself, HA (in your face Dad!).

I posted a comment the other day, and all it said was handle every stressful situation like me (a dog) - if you can't eat it or play with it, then piss on it and walk away HA. That bad boy got 30 likes, must be a lot of stressed-out people. You all need to chill, folks! Like me, I am going now for a snooze. Be back in a mo.

I've had a little snooze, but again it was interrupted, can't a dog get some downtime? Jeez, Louise! Anyhow, the racket that woke me was some funky-sounding music, it was all jangly and howling. I thought, this is my kind of sound, people.

I went to check it out, apparently it's called country music, and the particular song that woke me was by someone called Johnny Cash, it's called "I Walk the Line". Wowzers! Man, I was tapping my paw and waggling my tail to that tune, it was a pure delight to my ears, not like some of the crap out there now that gets played on the radio, all boom, boom, boom crap!

No, this was music where you could understand the blooming words for starters, and it made me feel great, in fact I think I would've been a great cowboy. A Stetson, and some spurs, yeah I can see it now, gun fight at the Ole Dog Corral. I'm gonna check in that catalogue to see if I can find me a cowboy hat…

Back in a mo…

Well unfortunately people, I can't get a hat, however I have tweeted a pic of myself with a cowboy outfit on (photoshopped) and I think it broke the internet. HA, in your face Kim somebody or other, whatever your name is, people would rather see a dawgie dressed as a cowboy.

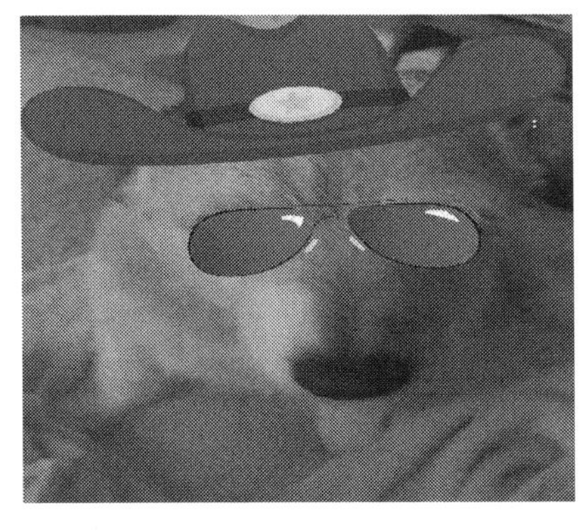

I now have 60 followers and I can tell you, some folks are pretty weird! I might have to block a few, I mean who tweets naked pics of themselves with their dogs hiding their genitals, seriously people, NOBODY wants to see that, especially if your dog is like a Chihuahua! HA.

It's dark out and I need food and a snooze, so bye for now…

Oh, some stats:

Treats: ZERO (I still feel hurt after Dad's comments)

Birds stared at: 5 (boring sparrows)

Pigeon Bastards barked at: 2 (winged rats are back, cooing)

Chapter Four - Weirdos, Froggy and a Bed

Wednesday

GO AWAY, I have had it with these early starts. I am not getting out of this warm bed, it's dark, it's goddam freezing cold and I am just too snuggly.

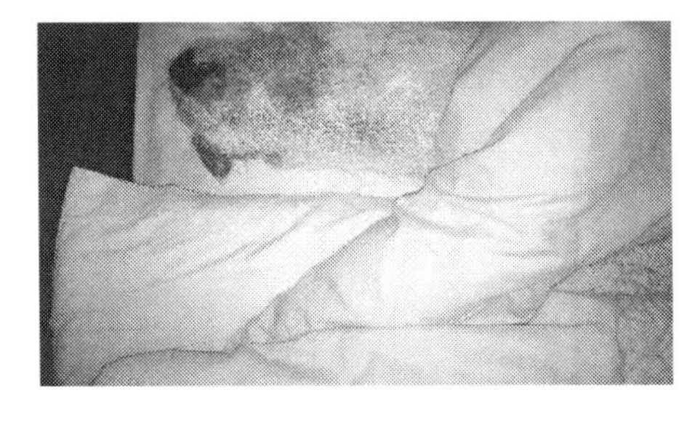

Oh to hell with it, I can smell food, this means now I have no choice but to get up, do I? Mum has done this on purpose, I just know it.

It's actually my favourite I can smell, toast. You can't beat a bit of toast and cup of tea in the mornings, especially when it's this cold. Autumn is certainly upon us people, however I'm not looking forward to November, NO, NO, NO, fireworks, HATE, HATE, HATE them, but for now I don't want to even think about it, we are several weeks away yet. At the moment we have Halloween to contend with, and all them greedy, begging little munters that come knocking, but I soon see them away HA.

Anyway, TOOOASSST! Gimme, gimme, gimme… right, I have been sitting now, longingly looking at Mum, for 10 minutes and she has not relented once, what's the deal? "Why aren't you looking at me?"

Hey, "Are you looking at me?" (HA De Niro's back)… Oh oh oh she's turning her head, it's happening, here it comes, come to poppa, toast pieces, OH YEAH BABY, she actually saved me a couple of pieces! Oh I love, love, love you Mum! P.S. DO NOT tell Dad! Life is wondrous.

Well folks, I have to go for my walk, so be back soon.

I'M BACK, and I can't believe what I saw, either. Dummy Douglas is insane, seriously, he's only gone and had all his fur shaved off, in this freaking cold! I shouted to him, "Hey Douglas, what gives? It's me, Rupert", and instead of his usual bark, bark, bark, you know what the daft eejit said back? He said his Dad hadn't bathed him for two months, two whole freaking months, and, as he is white, he was starting to resemble a vagrant, so, rather than cleaning him, his Dad shaved off all his freaking fur.

I said, "Man, that's ruff!" Ha Ha, no seriously I said, "your Dad sounds as stooped as you then, Douglas". Oh he didn't like that! Bark, bark, bark, bark. I was like yeah, yeah, piss off.

I live around some crazy characters, of course there's the usual crowd you know about now, Ian Beagle, Pomerbitch, Ginger Bastard, Bassett, and now there is another newbie. I can't keep up with this lot, and all that extra sniffing… Anyway this newbie has a face like a squashed arse, goddam, I thought, you can keep that face away from my rear, urggghh! I did shout a hello, and he was all like murmuring and shit. I said I can't hear you, I can't understand what you are saying… I gave up in the finish. If I pass him again, I shall try and find out what he is, but for now, he was small, and tan, with a mushed-up face. Maybe he had an accident and ran into a wall, I don't know, but goddam, people, I truly live near some right weirdos.

So it's Wednesday and not a lot is happening. I call it hump day, as we are halfway through the week, so halfway over the hill to the weekend, see, get it? NO? piss off then. So boring really, in fact I am so bored that I might have to have a snooze (I did warn you I am sedate, old and fat).

Bye for now…

I am back, I only had a quick siesta, because I suddenly remembered something that could entertain me, and that's my serial killer patch. I haven't been out to it for a while, last time was to bury Froggy No Eyes, so off I went to have a mooch.

Shock, horror, Froggy No Eyes - is still there. Ha, did you think I was going to say something like he had dug himself out? Don't be freaking stupid! But he has gone a little mouldy and smells a bit rank to be honest, eurgh he doesn't taste so nice anymore either. I need to have him washed I think to re-bury him, I'm going to take him back in to Mum, and see if she will wash him. If I drop him at her feet and do my whiny dance, I think she will get the message. Wish me luck, I'm doing it…

Well people, that was a disaster! Not only did Mum screech obscenities at me (and seriously my ears bled), she grabbed hold of Froggy No Eyes and wrapped him in a plastic bag (he might suffocate, people!) and then put him back in the bin! I am distressed, this was not the plan. Froggy No Eyes is no more! I have to accept this. I shall say a few words. "Froggy Froggy no-eyed bastard, kept me happy in times of woe, started life as a greeneyed king, ended up as a chewed-up thing". HA, that should do, RIP Froggy No Eyes.

I am going to have to find something new to bury in my patch now, to fill the gap left by Froggy. Ooooohhh what can I bury? I know, I know, I know, I've freaking got it, I am off to get it…

Well people I am a genius, I have buried one of my dental sticks! Now when I am feeling a little peckish, all I have to do is mosey on out to my patch and dig that bad boy up, HA! This much thinking and handsomeness has made me tired, so off now for a little nappy wappy…

Oh before I go, stats:

Treats: 2 (back to my normal self)

Birds stared at: 7 (one was a robin again, I like them)

Pigeon bastards barked at: 1 (he actually flew into the window! how retarded is he? Ha Ha Ha)

Thursday

My body is sooooo stiff today Diary, I think it must have been all that digging and burying yesterday. Oh yeah, I nearly forgot I have a hidden dental stick. I might fetch that later.

Well, best get up and stretch out this fat little body. I like to pretend I can do yoga, my favourite position being downward facing dog, obviously. Oh come on people, you have to give me that. I mean it is early and already the jokes are a-flowing. I reckon I could do stand up, if there was a stage short enough for me to get onto, boom, boom.

Just checked Twitter, no real activity to report, no new followers. That can't be right, surely the Internet must be broken, I'm gonna check again. No, nothing, nada, that's depressing, maybe I have lost my sparkle. I need some new material. I shall have to spend today, Diary, coming up with new ideas to gain attention.

I have just got back from my walk, yes same old, same old. I can't be bothered to mention it today, but something interesting occurred, and it might be news for Twitter. On the way back we spotted a delivery driver outside my house, and I thought, here we go again, parcel for eejit face next door, but NO, hang on, he is waiting for us! Of course I barked like mad, just in case he couldn't see me. And Mum shouted, "hang on, just let me get in".

Well, well, well, Diary, you are not gonna believe this, it's a parcel for me, ME, ME, ME, the amazing ME! You want to know what it is, people? It's a brand new bed! Oh, how wonderful… whoa, hang on…

WTF, a new bed, what does this mean, are they trying to oust me out of theirs? They can piss off if they think I am sleeping in a bed ON MY OWN, no way, no freaking way people, NO!

But, oooo I've tried it, it's soft, it's round, it's comfy. It still does not mean I am getting in it for night night time, NO. I love my sleepy night times with Mum and Dad, it's the only time of the day when I get them both together properly for snuggly wuggly times, and it's bliss. I even get to sleep at the top of the bed in between them, and then I kind of like to stretch my legs (stumps) out as far as they will go to make a bit more space for myself. I mean seriously how much goddam room do they need.

So I AM NOT, repeat NOT, getting in that freaking thing for sleepy times. I might venture in it during the day, or perhaps when they are watching something scary on the TV, but that is it, people.

I need food now, the stress of this situation has unbalanced me. I am off to forage and see what slim pickings Mum has, she better have something good after this fiasco.

I am back briefly, I had some lovely chewy duck fillet thing, tasted nicer than it sounds, so it made up for the drama earlier. However, I admit I did try lying in the new bed for a little afternoon snooze fest, and it was as comfy as hell on my joints. Maaaann, it was like lying in a giant marshmallow, still NOT for sleepy night time though, OK.

So treats today: 1 (the duck thing, nice)

Birds stared at: 8 (I wish they would do a bit more with their lives)

Pigeon bastards barked at: 4 (they were active today

Friday

Friday = shopping = new treats, whoop whoop… I am up and ready for action today, as Dad is off, and as you know he goes shopping today, and so I have to practice my best "what you got for me?" dance.

It involves lots of spinning round on one spot and compulsory squeaks.

Before all the action though I have checked my Twitter, as yesterday I tweeted a pic of MOI in my new bed, just for the ladies! And, guess what, it has already had 35 likes, and 5 more new followers! So I am back, this is what people want to see, a handsome dude, just chilling in his new bed. I shall have to take a few more shots, of different poses, maybe with me cuddling my stuffed KK, that should get some attention, yeah that's what I shall do. But for now, walkies, I hear the lead.

Back from my walk. I said to Douglas, "hey Baldy", just to see if he noticed it was me, Rupert, but no, back to not recognising me! Woof, woof, woof, woof, woof, he seriously is a dumb bastard. I might start going out with a sign round my neck saying "It's Rupert, and this is my mum!" Also spotted the newbie again, and I now know what he is people, he's a pug (he's seriously ugly, that's what he is), but at least I've found out, and managed to get some sense out of him today! His owner looks a bit squashed-up mush-faced as well, ha, ha, ha, I think I will call them the PUGLY CLUB!

Well Dad is back from shopping, and yee hah, it's time for the dance! I am killing it today, just killing it, I am like super squeaky and cute, and it's freaking worked, Dad has just produced the biggest bag of treats, and he is handing me one! It looks like a chewy stick, but the smell, oh the smell is roast chicken people, and it's moist and chewy, and chewy and moist, oh I said that, did I say it's chewy, I am off running, running, running with my chewy stick (udders bouncing)… Be back soon (nom nom nommmmmm nommmm)…

That was chewtastic, I actually slobbered over myself and had a bit of dribble in my beard. Did I care? did I bollocks, I want another one. I wonder, if I give my Dad the big sad-eyed look I give my Mum, will he relent? I'm off to try, wish me luck…

You are not going to believe this people, it bloody worked! I sloped into the kitchen all ninja style and just hung around his legs a bit, sniffing, looking cute, and then to get his attention I nudged his leg a bit. He looked down and said, "what's wrong my boy, you want some Dad love?" I thought, "NO f***ing way, I want another treat, dick weasel!"

But what I actually telepathically said was, "yes please Daddy, love me, stroke me (not the face), and please give me another chewy treat", and then BAM, out popped another chewy stick! Dad said "is this what you want, my little fatty?", but of course by this point he could call me whatever the hell he wanted, so I did my squeaky dance and he stuffed that stick right in my mouth! Off I went, waddling into the lounge, to be in chewy stick heaven. Nom nom nom, see you in a second!

Ppfffffttt, oops excuse me, oh freaking hell I can't even sit by me with that smell! Jesus, if we had a cat I could blame him, it must be the chewy sticks. Anyway, I suppose it's time I told you why I don't like my face being messed with!

It was when I was younger and more agile, and we were out for an evening walk, when this older couple passed by and stopped to talk to my Mum. Next thing I know the old pissy bag woman has leant down to talk to me, and starts rubbing my face with her gloved hands (it was winter and cold) and these gloves are the fffing woollen type, and seriously they are really irritating my face, but she won't stop, and she's making this ridiculous sound, all oooooos and awwwws and he's a lovely pup, and because I was on my lead contraption and couldn't escape I had to freaking sit there and endure this, until finally I couldn't deal with it anymore, I snapped people, yes that's right, I growled at her and bared my teeth at the old pissy crow, just to warn her, but did it? NO… She carried on and said "oh Mr Grumpy Chops", well that was it, I bit her finger, didn't draw blood thankfully, because of her STOOPID ITCHY woollen gloves, but I thought PISS OFF, you asked for that.

Well of course I was an embarrassment, so Mum said, and I was lucky she didn't press charges, oh whatever! So from then on, nobody was allowed to touch me, especially when we were out walking, and if it happened again I would be muzzled. I thought, bollocks, even if I do look like Hannibal Lecter, so from now on, nobody touches the face, capiche? So that is the reason, I am not bad, just cantankerous, and anyway like I said she asked for it, the old wrinkley.

All this talk of yesteryear has tired me out, so I am off for a snooze…

I am awake and on HIGH Alert, alert, alert, alert, stranger danger! We have a visitor and this is highly unusual, as Mum doesn't like folks in the house (other than Nanny Hammy or Potato, yes it's weird I know, but it's the way she is)… Anyway, this person I can hear has a gruff voice, I need to go and investigate this people, back soon…

Well freaking hell, this is weird, it's a man and he knows Dad, and he has a very strange smell about him! With my bionic nose I could smell oil, petrol, snakes, birds, and cheese and onion! (Yuk!) (not to the cheese bit obvs!)

Apparently, he is a mechanic and he had come to see about repairing some fault on Dad's car, so that explains the oil and petrol smells. However god only knows what the snake and bird smells are that I've picked up! Truly weird, I need to see if I can investigate further, back in a mo…

I have found out folks what the strange smells are, he owns snakes, for real, goddam snakes, what kind of weirdo owns reptiles? Only one kind of best friend a man needs people, and that's a dog. Oh and he has an African Grey Parrot that swears more than me! I would like to meet this bird, what a conversation, at least he would be more entertaining than the bloody sparrows and pigeons I see day in day out. The cheese and onion were crisps he had eaten for his lunch (yuk again).

Anyway, reptiles. NO, NO, NO, and he has them in tanks in his lounge, I heard him say. F**k that, what if they escaped one night, and started slithering over your face? ARRGGGHHH I have just been reminded of black snake Mr Harvey! Oh god I need a lie down, I might have to go in my bed, a secure haven, yes alright judging bastards I hear you, "oh he likes his bed now", well I yes do, PISS OFF, I still get to sleep with Mum and Dad at night night time, so in your face.

Anyway…

Treats today: 4 (the smelly man had to give me two, to stop me growling at him)

Birds stared at: 8 (boring sparrows, about time they got a life)

Pigeon bastards barked at: 3 (irritating winged rats)

Saturday

I slept for 12 hours straight after the reminder of the snake fiasco and the horror it conjured up. I still cannot imagine why anyone would want a reptile. It's not even got any fur for you to stroke, eurrggghhh, they are all bald and shiny, in fact that's like my Granddad (Potato Head). Ha, Ha, Ha. Maybe he was related to a snake at some point.

Well folks, it's Saturday, oh yeah, oh yeah, and so far I have had plenty of snuggly wuggly from both Mum and Dad this morning in their bed, it was heaven! Then they kicked me out for some strange reason and now I am downstairs in the lounge ON MY OWN! This is odd…

I can now hear strange grunting sounds! I am going back up to investigate… I think Mum is hurt, oh god my eyes, my eyes, I did not want to see that! WTF man, why would Dad be doing that to my Mum, I tried climbing on the bed to stop him, I think he's trying to kill her! And again he looks red, and is it raining out? I have to go back downstairs, I am going in my marshmallow bed, the safe place. I shall report back later.

Well 3 minutes have gone by! And, Mum is now downstairs!! Thank god that's over (it must be an anniversary or something!) but my Dad is not an athlete, unlike MOI!! Ha, ha, come on people you love this comedy, anyway time for food, gimme, gimme, gimme my breakfast.

Oooo what delights have we got this morning, oooh I am smelling beef and biscuits, that's new, I hope it's not that dry crappy stuff again and I hope she's not trying to diet me again because she can just piss right off, NOOOOOOO, OK? Otherwise you're gonna learn about loss (ha De Niro's back)… Well people, I have tried this "new" food and it's not too bad - it was moist and chewy but crunchy at the same time (genius really how they perfect it), but still it was missing my favourite sausage pieces, so may have to feign disgust so Mum doesn't keep serving me the same shit day in day out, just like poor Dad who the other day I heard moaning about his packed lunch.

He said something like "why is it when I say I like something, I then get it for the next month?" Mum answered with some obscenity or other and told him to make his own pissing sandwiches from now on, so she obviously has a tendency to repeat things! HA

So I've checked Twitter, and you are going to be astounded, I now have 80 followers, That is super amazing people! I posted another pic of myself in my bed but I was posed on my back with my udders out, I was like somebody milk these bad boys, it had over 40 likes, like I said a lot of weirdos out there!

Well I need a little snooze, it is Saturday after all and seeing as now Dad is resting again (must have been the 3 minutes of activity!), I am off to lie with him for a change, and prepare myself for the begging munters later.

Treats so far: zero (I know, I need to have a word)

Birds stared at: also zero! (troubling)

Pigeon Bastards barked at: zero (something is off)

Chapter 5 - Begging Munters, Lost and Found

I have slept for almost 5 hours - that was awesome. Dad even cuddled me and said I was a good boy, so I have decided to forgive him for his horrible fat comments. Well it's dark out now, the nights are drawing in since the clocks went back, so can't see shit out! Oh I can, wait a minute, WHY is there another dog who looks just like me in MY garden? I need to ward him off! I am going to bark, shit, it's not working, he is still there, and I swear he is the double of me! Oh hang on people, I feel as dumb as Douglas

, it IS me, ha, ha, ha. It's just my reflection in the patio glass, but hey, how handsome am I, eh? Eh? Anyway, I have to go for a walk, seeing as how neither of my parents could be bothered this morning, that's neglect - I will ring that show one of these days, and speak directly with that Paul guy, that will show 'em. But still, we are here, we go, see you in a mo, ooo I am a poet and I didn't know it… Ha, killing it today people, just killing it.

Just got back from my walk, and as I say it's dark out, but as I am THE bionic dog, my eyesight is better than any human's out there. I don't need to eat carrots or shit, I have super see-in-the-dark eyes, and boy did I see a lot of crazies out tonight, I bet any money they will be knocking on our door very soon.

Oh here we go, here are the first begging munters of the night. I mean seriously why can't Mum or Dad put up a sign that simply says "Munters DO NOT STOP HERE, piss off", but NO, they like to get in the spirit of Halloween, no consideration for me, well I am going to ruin it as per usual. I am off to ward off the first lot, back in a mo…

That did not go as planned, in fact I was so scared by the costumes I actually farted (one of them was dressed as a clown, I pissing hate clowns, super weird), and the smell! It was like blocked drains, so it soon drove them away ha, in your face begging bastards… Oh dear god that's the door again, when will this end, I am so sick of it already, I need to bark more, I'm going for it…

My bark was mighty this time and I was prepared for the scary costumes, but this lot had planned better and they had a little treat for me, so of course I was all like doe eyed and cute looking… Still Mum warned them not to touch my face, as they risked losing one of their midget munter fingers, which to me look like tiny edible sausages, oooohh sausage pieces, yum yum come to poppa… sorry drifted a bit there, I must never bite the hands that feed me.

I am going to check Twitter again, all this door knocking is causing havoc with my digestion, ppppffffftttt oops sorry, must have been one of the munters' treats that didn't agree with me. I know, I am going to photoshop myself as a pumpkin and put the caption as "Pump Fiction", ha ha ha! Oh I do amuse myself.

The picture was a hit people, 53 likes to that beauty, oh I cannot wait for Christmas, the pics

I can create, in fact I could do a calendar, I am that cute. Oh Jesus H. Christ there is the door again, needs must, woof, woof, woof, woof, woof, let's see what this bunch of munters wants.

The sweet sickly voices of 'em go right through me, "trick or treat", well trick then, begging munters! Ha that's fooled ya ain't it, don't know what to do now, that's because you are all greedy bastards, and out for what you can get.

Oh dear god, one of them has started to cry… FFS, he is saying to his friend that he is going to tell his Mum, as his friend got all the good sweets and if he doesn't share, he is in trouble. Listen up kid, never rat on your friends and always keep your mouth shut (De Niro classic). I don't think he heard me though, as he is off running to his Mummy, what a big baby munter, this is why I don't like rug rat begging munter bastards. I need a lie down - this has exhausted me.

If the door goes again this evening I am going to give one of them my buried dental stick, ha, see if they like that! They won't come again. I am off to curl up in my comfy bed as Mum and Dad keep having to get up and down, serves them right.

It has finally gone peaceful, so must be past the begging munters' bedtime, thank god. I can now get up on the sofa and snuggle next to my Mum, hopefully there will be some good show on the TV, I hope it's Game of Thrones again. I love that show, I would be a great night watchman.

Well it isn't Game of Thrones, it's Strictly, but I do love glitter, I think in fact I could do with a new sparkly collar, just to set my eyes off. I might have to check the catalogue, I am thinking red leather with some diamante studs, yes that would look super cool. Then that broad Pomerbitch would be all up in my face and I could say "wow broad, you talkin' to me?" Ha ha, I told you I am hilarious.

I am starving, I don't know what's up with me, it must have been watching all that dancing, it's made me ravenous, so I need to do some serious staring, starting NOW…

I am doing it, I am looking intently at Mum and I am making my special whiny bark noise, a bit of a poke with my paw on her thigh, yes that should do it. Oh she's looking at me, oh oh oh she's getting off the sofa and YES, she's walking to the kitchen. I must follow…

I am at her feet. She's making a cup of tea, I think, but I will not give up, time to pull out the little whiny dance, front paw stomping move, here goes… Oh yeah baby she is reaching into the treat cupboard, and she is pulling out a green thing, WTF, this is new (more new stuff!), oh but it's shaped like a dental stick, oh it's minty, I likey, I am off skipping to the lounge to nom nom nommm on my new dental stick thing. If I get one of these again I will call them my grass sticks, ha! (Not like marijuana, people! I am not a drug addict, no, grass as in it's green like grass, you dopes HA dopes!)

OH Yeah baby that was delicious, and it helped clean my teeth so double whammy bonus. I need to check my Twitter, but my eyes feel heavy, I will just have a little snooze and then get to it.

Yes, yes, alright I have slept through again and it's Sunday, so what, in fact it's super cold out so I may have to stay wrapped up in the quilt all day. Oh hell, nooooooooo, Mum is calling me, why is she up this early on a Sunday, it's only 7am! Get a life woman… I have to go, be back in a mo… Well that was interesting people, when I finally got downstairs, after grooming myself, and doing my best break dance moves over the bed {I love doing that when it's empty, I just roll and scoot around and around on the giant bed, it's ace, anyway sorry, I have wandered again, it's my mind), Mum was in the kitchen and she actually had some cheese out. I thought this is odd, it's not summer, I don't have itchy skin, so what gives?

Well folks it was a tablet, but not any type you really want, so all your fellow dawgies out there be warned, this was for worms! I actually spat the tablet bit out, and just ate the cheese, in your face Mum, you can't fool me! But WTF, she is picking it up, OH MY GOD, she is shoving it down my throat, and massaging under my chin at the same time, I can't escape people, somebody call for help, this is wrong! OH thank Christ that's over, I have swallowed it (note to self NEVER be fooled by that again), seriously I don't have worms living inside me, that is so disgusting, just the thought of that has made me want to have a lie down, but NO we are off for a walk now, I can hear my no-fun bungee rattling, back soon.

Ha, ha, ha, ha, I am splitting my sides, and it's not because Dad is in his badminton gear again. No this is even funnier people, on my walk some daft bastards have gone and lost their cat, and it's Ginger Bastard (that's not the funny part, I am not a sadist). No, the funny part is that they have gone and put up posters, but they look hand drawn as if by some retard kid, and seriously it looks nothing like Ginger Bastard, I think I could've done a better drawing. It's like a blind Picasso has drawn it, I am actually wetting myself, they are never gonna find Ginger Bastard with that.

I seriously hope Ginger Bastard is alive and well though. Even if I hate him, he was my entertainment some mornings, come home soon you ginger bastard if you are out there.

Well I am checking my Twitter, let's see what the world of weirdos has to say, oooooo now this is interesting, I am being followed by a cat, but he is not a real cat, he is a stuffed doorstop. HA HA, this is hilarious, I mean as if a doorstop can speak and type, it's got no hands for starters!

But still, who am I to judge, it's one more follower, I think I might engage with this doorstop and see what he or she has to say....

Well I sent a tweet to the doorstop and it's a "she", ridiculous, and her name is, get this, Stuffed Bastard - that is quite ingenious really, and very funny. Better watch that this stuffed creation doesn't steal my limelight, in fact no fear of that as I have posted another pic of myself in my serial killer patch again and people love it.

Oh yeah, I forgot to say I had a wander out there, briefly, yesterday to my patch and checked on my buried items. Some of them are smelling a bit rank! I might have to dig up Monkey Boy and get him washed, but shall leave him perhaps through the winter. I shall have a think about it. So back to the pic, I had this cute look on my face and I was mid-dig with my paw in the dirt, and my caption was "ooo I could fit three bodies in here!" Ha, ha, that got over 60 likes, like I say an awful lot of crazy folks out there! But as long as they don't start stalking me, it's all good.

I need a snooze, so I am off to lay with Mum, as Dad has decided he is still doing this badminton malarkey. Personally it seems far too energetic for me as I like sedate, but that's his preference. Oh before I go, funny story: when Dad was younger some years ago, he did embark on a fitness routine and he went all out, he even bought a machine that you could run on, but go nowhere (bit stupid really, why not just run outside?).

Anyway, he used this machine daily for about 4 weeks. It was in the dining room and it used to face the outside patio doors, so the back of it was close to the dining room wall, which at the time had this stuff on it called Artex, used to add texture, but I think only should have been on a ceiling! (It's ugly and hard and has sharp edges!) Anyway, there he was running away to his music (80's, quite good stuff) and he decides to turn up the pace of this machine, thinking he was like Seb Coe or somebody like that… I was lying on the sofa at the time, and I heard this whizzing fast sound, along with a quick pounding sound, and thought WTF, so I ran to the dining room (it was when I could run fast) and there was Dad, very odd in colour, like beetroot red, and dripping wet, again I thought has it been raining inside? but it was his legs that fascinated me, they were trying to keep up with this machine and unfortunately the machine was winning, and then it happened people!

This machine flung my Dad off at such a pace, he hit the Artex wall with such a force some of it fell off! I thought, my god, he is dead, there was blood and grazed skin and bruising, so I did what any good dog would do and ran over to my Dad and started to lick the blood off his arm and check he was ok, this was of course after laughing hysterically with my Mum, who had come running in from the kitchen when she heard the commotion. I tell you people I have never seen my Mum laugh so much (I think she is a sadist!) and Dad was very angry and his language was horrific, thank the lord he was ok and the only real injury was his pride, whatever that is!

Let's just say, the running machine was sold the next week, as Dad deemed it far too dangerous and that was the end of his fourth fitness attempt. I shall elaborate on the other three another day, as for now I really do need a nap, so see you in a mo.

I am back, that was a really good nap, me and Mum snuggled close together on the sofa with a blanket. I was boiling under it, but didn't care as I was with Mum. Dad came back from badminton and he looked a lot happier, I heard Mum say "you must be getting better", and Dad said "Yeah I actually won today", so I think he is happy, and this might be the sport for him, genteel and pussy-like!

Oh, this is strange, I can hear Nanny Hammy and Granddad Potato… What are they doing here on a Sunday? I am going to investigate…

Well, well, well, this is interesting, they have come for lunch, the begging bastards! Ha joking, I love my Nanny and Granddad, they give me nice treats, in fact Nanny Hammy pulled out a mouthwatering chewy chicken stick, and it was divine, nom nom nommm, so they can stay. In fact if they are here for lunch I wonder if Mum is making beef! OMG if she does, this will make my day, I need to go and see…

It's NOT beef, people, however it is roast chicken, which is my second favourite, so I must perfect my dance if I am to get any of that. With Nanny Hammy here it could be slim pickings, as she likes to eat all the pies! Constantly hungry she is, in fact she is worse than me (do not tell her any of this!).

The other week she came round on a Monday, as she does (oh, so she will be here again tomorrow, eating my food) - she gorged herself on seven chocolate biscuits. I sat drooling over her lap, I even licked her hand, but I got given none, as unfortunately people dogs can't be given chocolate - it's poisonous, along with grapes, for some strange reason, but who would want to eat them funny oval things is beyond me.

Anyway, it seems that before lunch we are all embarking on a walk to the park. Whoo hoo people, I can do some duck terrorising, I am off! See you later, alligator…

That was some terrorising, I waddled in there among them duck bastards and they were giving it their all, that quack, quack, quacking getting more and more high pitched… I said "come on boys, you quacking at me?" Ha, ha, I am the king of comedy.

However, what is even bigger news, is that the posters for Ginger Bastard have been taken down, which leads me to believe he has been found safe and well, or, well you don't need me to tell you the alternative (let's just say there are lots of Chinese restaurants round here!). I need to investigate, and find out if Ginger Bastard is alive. Be back in a mo…

People the news is good, Mum bumped into Ginger Bastard's owner and she said that he was trapped in some neighbour's shed, and when the neighbour went to get his golf clubs out there he was, meowing and shit, pussy bastard. At least he was in a warm place, anyway he is back home now and I can look forward to my morning entertainment again.

All this drama and walking has made me sleepy, I think I need another little snooze. I shall check Twitter later and hopefully when I wake there will be a roast chicken dinner for me.

I can hear carving, or am I dreaming? No, no, definitely carving, I must jump up quickly out of this slumber and go and see… (The quickly bit is a joke ok?) I actually rolled out of my prostrate position sedately, yawned and stretched my bulging udders out, and wandered to the kitchen.

Yeah people, the table is laid, Nanny Hammy and Granddad potato are seated, and my bowl is on the side and I can smell the most divine-smelling roast chicken EVER. In fact I can even smell potatoes (no we are not eating Granddad), they are roasted lovely little new potatoes that Mum makes and they are lip-smacking lovely, yum yum, nom nom nom, come on serve it bitch, I mean Mum.

"Heaven, I'm in heaven, la, la, la la"… That was scrummy and yummy and I actually gobbled it up in 30 seconds flat, and now I am seated by Nanny Hammy doing my little grape dance, hoping beyond hope there will be leftovers. In fact with Nanny's record, I have no chance, so I'm going to sit next to Mum, she always relents.

Ppppfffffffftttt, oh excuse me, must be the roast chicken… Ha ha Granddad Potato has just farted as well at the table and Nanny Hammy is swearing again, she is calling him a disgusting dirty old man! Glad it's not just me that has loose bowels, he does stink. Phew wheeeee! That has actually put me off wanting any more, I need a snooze, but before I go, I will check Twitter. No real activity, everyone must be having a lazy Sunday.

See you people, it could be a while, all that roast chicken and carbs…

P.S. not looking forward to next week. Bonfire HELL…

Chapter 6 - Bonfire Hell and a Hedgehog

Monday has come round again, yes, yes I slept through, big deal, it was too cosy and warm and I just couldn't keep my eyes open. Anyway, I think Nanny Hammy is here, so I am off to say hello again, and see if she has any treats like yesterday.

Well Nanny did have a treat for her favourite Numero Uno grandson (she doesn't have any other grandsons) and it was a delicious cheesy bone! I don't know why Mum can't get nice treats like these, I am going to have to have a word. Same old shit she gets, no wonder Dad complains about his packed lunch so much, I get it now.

I am being called - it's walkies time, so be back shortly…

Well that didn't take long. Apparently Nanny Hammy can't walk
very well today, her hips were hurting her. Must have been the walk yesterday, tired her out, or it's all the roast chicken she ate and now it's

resting on her hips! (Note to self, do not let Nanny read this…) I think she needs my special diet of dry crappy food stuff, that should sort her out! Mind you she would probably like it, she eats almost anything.

We did see Ginger Bastard and I laughed in his face, and shouted "Get locked in any sheds lately, pussy bastard? I heard you were a crying ball of fur!" Oh he didn't like that, took a right good swipe at me, but fortunately Mum pulled me in on my bungee!

I tell you something though, there were new posters up for some big bonfire thing on Wednesday, and I am NOT looking forward to that at all. I really, really, really hate fireworks night, and a few years back it was horrendous. Mum and Dad tried to get me to go to a display, something about "face your fears" shit, like the more I am exposed to the sounds and loud bangs, the more I am supposedly desensitised to them. Did it work? I hear you say. DID IT F**K!!! I was an absolutely terrified bag of nerves, in fact I don't think I have quite forgiven them, however there was a funny bit to the story.

We got to the display before they had lit the fire and so I was having a good old mooch around, sniffing anything and everything. Then we got close to the bonfire, which was stacked up with old wood and stuff, well then something piqued my interest. I could smell something curious, which was lurking about under a pile of leaves close to the bonfire.

I started squeaking and whining and I was pulling on my bungee for all I was worth, when finally I managed to break free. I scurried right to the pile of leaves and OMG, I have never ever seen anything like this before, so of course I was delighted! It was round, like a football, but it also had spikes, and it moved when I nudged it. I was in squeaky heaven.

By this time Mum wanted to know what all the commotion was and came running over. To my horror and Dad's, she yanked me so fast back on my lead I swear to god I nearly choked and started to do this yakking sick sound. Did Mum care? NO, she seemed more interested in this spiky ball. I thought FFS, it's just a ball, but no people it was not just a ball, it was a thing called a hedgehog!.

I had never even heard of this creature, but apparently at this time of the year they look for somewhere to hibernate and you have to be really careful where bonfires are concerned otherwise you could roast them, which in all fairness would not be very nice, but I suppose it could have been a new addition to my serial killer patch! Too much? oh piss off, it was a spiky fleabag, because yes they have fleas… Anyway, Mum was all like concerned and shit, and said it needed to be moved away from the bonfire before it was lit, so she called an attendant who helped her scoop him up and put him to safety.

She was so smug-looking and proud, like she had done such a good deed, but it was ME who found the flea-ridden bastard, so I don't know why nobody ever thanked me, but they didn't. All I got was a telling-off for trying to pick it up and toss it in the air!

So, back to the actual display and the desensitisation technique. There we were, waiting for the fireworks to start, and at first I thought, this isn't so bad. It was warm with the heat of the now-lit bonfire, and the smells were divine, a combination of sugar, donuts, potatoes, beef and yummy sausages, so I was in smell heaven, or hell actually as I couldn't eat any of it.

Then it started, whizz, bang, whizzzzzzzzz, and my ears! Good god, it was horrendous, how humans do not all end up deaf I have no idea… Then the loud bomb-like bangs started, I was so traumatised, my tail had disappeared up my arse, and my farts were abysmal, the smell was rancid! Mum and Dad realised that their technique was actually not going to work, and so quickly scooped me up and carried me back to the car, by which point I was omitting a strange smell from my body. My anal glands had released their potent stress odour and it filled the car. All I can say is, the journey back home was a long and smelly one, and it was all Mum and Dad's fault, bastards.

When we finally got home I was so relieved, but still suffering such severe trauma that I had to immediately evacuate my bowels on the front lawn. I said "clean that bad boy up Mum, serves you right".

So now every bonfire night I go into a state of panic and I have to go through a safe routine, which involves plug-in calming things, a blanket (not the special vet one), treats, music and closed curtains. It is HELL.

But for now I am ok, I have until Wednesday to prepare, so I am going to check on Twitter to see if any of my furry companions are having to face the same misery.

The Twitterverse has gone mental, all the furry ones are complaining and saying the same - that they are not looking forward to Bonfire Night - and in fact someone is petitioning for fireworks to be banned. I agree, in fact I have signed that petition, and retweeted it.

Stuffed Bastard has tweeted a pic of her sitting by the door with an empty carton of food, and the caption says "Stuffed out",Ha she is amusing, I like this broad, I think we could be friends, however I am going to up my game…

HA in your face Stuffington, I have tweeted myself dressed as a Viking, with the caption, "You may take my followers, but you will never take my freedom"! Already it has 41 likes. I shall check back later, as for now I need a snooze. Nanny Hammy has gone now, probably as there are no biscuits left for her to gorge on, HA.

What a lovely snooze, Mum was very loving today… Probably feeling guilty because she knows Bonfire Night is nearly upon us and so is trying to sweettalk me, bitch got to do a lot more than just whisper sweet nothings, gimme food.

Oh she must have read my mind, I am being given one of my grass sticks, oh how lovely, fresh minty breath and a chewtastic treat all in one! Nom nom nommmmm, well that's a start.

We are going outside in the garden, time for a mooch and to check on my serial killer patch. I shall see if Monkey Boy needs to be dug up for a wash… Oh wait this is interesting, Mum is going in the greenhouse, she is not normally allowed in there as it's Dad's place, but she looks like she's cleaning it out… OMG I hope Dad hasn't left us and that's why she is in there! Oh no, it's ok folks, it's just time to clean it out for the winter. I have just heard her on the phone to Dad telling him her plans. Phew.

In fact this is fun for me, as I was never allowed in the greenhouse, either, after one incident, when I sneaked in. I know, sneaking and I just don't quite go in the same sentence, but anyhow, I crept in behind Dad, a few months back in the summer, and I could smell something so sweet and so divine that my mouth was drooling saliva. I just had to go and see what the smell was, and there hanging from tubs were these red gorgeous heart-shaped things.

I just had to have me some of them, so I craned my neck as far as it would go, and reached up to the tub with my mouth open… I ripped one of them bad boys off, but disaster, as I got hold of it in my mouth the whole of the tub came tumbling down on top of me and the soil was everywhere. Dad started shouting, "WTF get out Rupert, GET OUT!" I scurried out of there as fast as I could, but still had that juicy delight in my mouth, and boy it was yummy. I soon learnt that it was a strawberry, and yes we can have those in small quantities. It was delicious, it was sweet and yummy, but I had disturbed the plant and ruined it when the tub fell, so I was banished from the greenhouse and never allowed in when Dad was out there.

So today is exciting, I hope the strawberries are still there, I am off to investigate…

No strawberries people, they have long since ended, just empty tubs, and some old tomato plants that need throwing out. Mum has been busy cleaning and putting stuff away for the winter, so I have dug up Monkey Boy. I have taken him into the house for a wash, I hope Mum sees him and gets him clean, so I can get him reburied for the winter.

Oh wait what's this, I have found something interesting in the greenhouse, it looks like a hand… OMG I hope it's not real, tastes like soil though, ooo it's good to chew on, I am going to sit here for a while and chew it… Now Mum is shouting something, "Give me that back now!", I'm like "why? I want it"… Oh god she's coming for me, I shall run with it and hide it. She's still shouting, "Rupert give me that back, it's Dad's". Oh oh, I better drop it, I do not want to be in trouble with Dad for stealing anything else out of the greenhouse.

I found out what it was, it was one of his gardening gloves, which he uses when planting up. No wonder it tasted of soil, oh well, I didn't do it any harm. So Mum has gone inside and I can hear her from outside, screaming. I better go and see what all the fuss is about.

Oh she's found Monkey Boy. Calm down, it's only a bit of mould and dirt on him… She better get him washed, he is one of my favourites. I need to do the sad eye pleading look, I am whimpering now as well… Oh I think it's working, yes she is asking me, "do you want him washed Rupert?" Yes mother f**cker! I mean, "yes Mum please wash Monkey Boy". It's worked, she is actually putting him in the washing machine, YES results! I can now get him reburied when he comes out clean.

All that activity in the garden has made me sleepy, I think I will go and lie in my marshmallow bed for a bit, Mum can carry on outside. I need a snooze, so see ya later, mashed potato.

Woke up and checked Twitter, my pic has now had 57 likes.

I have tweeted about my escapades in the garden today and said I found a hand HA HA HA. People think I mean a real hand, idiots! Folks will believe anything. I must see who else I can follow, though, who else is funny like me… I mean I already follow Robert De Niro, he is my hero, but I need a new interest. I shall have to check out who is trending. I wish I could trend #tubbyfootstool, can you imagine the interest? I could go global, go to red carpet events, do interviews… I might even get to meet my hero

Robert, and I would be like, "are you talkin' to me?" "do I amuse you?" Oh god I am a comedy genius methinks.

I need to go and check on Monkey Boy now, see if he is nice and clean, so just gonna have a mosey on in to the kitchen, waddle, waddle, waddle, udders swinging, nearly there.

Oooooo, he's on the warm thing that I like to lie by sometimes, I think they are called radio haters or something like that, but that's a stupid name, as why would anything hate the radio? It plays cool sounds especially when it's on an 80's channel… Talking of which, the other day Mum was on her own, and the music was blaring, I think it was another country tune, Rhino stone cowboy or something like that (ha, named after me!). Anyway, she was doing this weird swaying motion in the lounge, I thought she was having some kind of episode, I nearly called for help, but then she started singing into Basil (my brush). I thought, wow this is super strange, what is she doing with Basil.

She had her eyes closed and I swear she really thought she sounded like the song, let me tell you people she DID NOT! It was actually a very strangled high-pitched sound she was emitting, and my ears nearly bled. I just had to stop her, so of course I started barking, but she took this as if I was joining in, as if! I had to stop her, so I waddled off and managed to grab Monkey Boy off the heating tin (much better name) and went and dropped him at her feet. This did halt the vicious assault on my ears, but she did not want to engage in play, she was too busy finishing the song, and then it got worse, she picked me up and started swaying with me in her arms to the tune! I thought WTF, I felt sick from all that side-to-side motion, but I couldn't wriggle free, and besides, it's quite a drop to the floor and I am NOT a cat, I do not land on all fours, rather it's more of a thumping thud, which happened once when I fell off the sofa, it's ok people I wasn't hurt, too much blubber.

Anyway, back to Monkey Boy. I need to get him outside so I can rebury him, let me go and scratch at the door and whine. Yes it's working, Mum is coming to let me out.

I am out people, I am a-digging and a-mooching and tossing the soil everywhere, this is so much fun, I love my serial killer patch! That looks like a deep enough hole now for Monkey Boy, in you go, I'll just nudge him a bit with my nose, yeah that's it, he's in, now time to put the soil back on him for winter. Oh I can hear Mum shouting at me, I think she is coming to check on my handiwork. I think she will be proud.

Noooooooooo, Mum was not impressed, she couldn't understand my logic of reburying Monkey Boy after she had washed him. DUH! He needed a freshening up, what is not to understand? Seriously, get a grip. Anyway, she has now gone and pulled him out of my patch and brushed him off… he is now sitting in my marshmallow bed, which I am not entirely happy about, but I shall have to leave him there for a day or two.

I have checked Twitter again and I now have 100 followers, people! That is epic, wowzers, it's the comedy, they just cannot get enough of me and my jokes. In fact here's one I posted the other day:

"What did the cat say when he lost all his money?"

"I'm paw!"

Sweary cat liked that, and fat cat, and even though I don't like cats, especially Ginger Bastard, those two are ok for cats.

Well, all this activity and mooching has made me exceptionally tired, so I am off for a nap, might even go and lie with Monkey Boy in the marshmallow bed…

Oh

Treats today: 3 (had to keep my energy levels up)

Birds stared at: 4(I think they are hibernating for winter)

Pigeon bastards barked at: 0 (good, piss off)

Wednesday

OMG people, I cannot believe I have missed a whole day! I seriously do not know how that happened, one minute I am all cosy in my bed with Monkey Boy snuggled up close to me (he is actually quite good company so might rethink the reburying of him), anyway, somehow I have woken up in the big bed, and I can hear Mum downstairs, and I think Dad has gone to do manly tasks at his job.

But anyhow, big bed all to myself again, this is bliss! I am going to ruffle the quilt and venture under it, whooo hooo, this is awesome, I can actually surf on these sheets. I am a-slipping and a-sliding, oh yeah baby, I need to roll around some more on my back, need to cover as much space on this bed as I possibly can. I need to make grunting sounds and snuffling sounds… Oh God this is heaven.

PEOPLE, PRESS THE PANIC BUTTON! I have just unfortunately realised that if I have missed a day, that means it's Wednesday and so bonfire night! Oh HELL, this is now the worst day ever. I am not getting out of this bed, no way, never, NO… Oh hang on Mum is shouting, I need to go to the top of the stairs. Oh, it's walkies time, I have to go, needs must and all that, back soon…

HA HA HA, the walk has cheered me up and taken my mind off the events for later. We passed another newbie, and he had shorter legs than mine - I wouldn't have thought it possible! This dude was like way, way stumpier than me, and not only that, he looked like - wait for it - A SAUSAGE! Yeah you heard me right people, a pissing sausage. I was mid-wee when he came pattering by, his little legs looked like that time my Dad was on his running machine, like they couldn't keep up, and his body was all stretched out and long, and brown, like a cooked hot dog sausage (Mum has those, yummy). Anyway I finished my wee and shouted, "yo, dude, where's your bun?" He actually thought that was quite funny, and he does have a good sense of humour for a German. Yes, he's German, people, and his name is Klaus, but I have nicknamed him Frankfurter! (oh come on people!) So another new face to say hi to, at least my walks are entertaining. We did pass Bassett, and Pomerbitch, but I ain't talking to that broad no more, too high maintenance and yappy for me. Then we passed Ginger Bastard, but he was too busy licking his arse to notice me, dirty bastard, so I didn't get to abuse him. All in all a good walk.

Back home now, and already I can feel the panic rising again. I really hope tonight is cancelled and it pisses it down with rain. That will teach the inconsiderate bastards who like to torture innocent animals and waste money. If you want to watch things blow up in the sky, go take yourselves up in a plane and jump out of it with sparklers up your arses! Sorry, rant over, I just hate fireworks.

Checked Twitter and it seems the consensus is the same, no one is looking forward to tonight. There were some good tips as well for keeping calm, one dawgie said, "have lots of treats by your side", I like the sound of that. In fact I don't think I am following him so will have to, he looks cool, all butch looking and manly, like me, Ha!

Well people, it's starting to get dark out. Dad is home and looks very tired. I think his job involves lots of heavy work, but Mum said something about, he only delivers stationery and ain't that pencils and pens and shit, so what a pussy, he needs to man up. His fitness attempts seem to be getting more and more genteel - his last effort in between badminton and the running machine escapade was golf. In fact Mum played with him, they used to go on a Sunday morning together, and Nanny Hammy would come round as sometimes Granddad potato would go with them.

But that has stopped now, something about how cold it is out and it's not the weather for golf… What are you lot, a bunch of ginger bastard pussies, afraid of a bit of cold? Man up, but bbbrrrrr it has turned a little chilly, might need to get under my blanket in preparation. Off for a little snooze, pppffftttttt, oh excuse me, it's the stress, about tonight.

Oh Jesus save me, please, I will promise to be nice to Ginger Bastard and never bark at the pigeons again… Oh Christ on a bike, what the hell, this has to be worse than any other previous year. The noises are so loud and they just will not stop. I need to run for cover, well waddle fast, I am going upstairs to the big bed. I've made it, I am in the big bed, but it's just as bad here, in fact I think it's worse, I am closer to the sky! I don't know what to do with myself, I am whining now and barking at the same time, in fact I am wharking… Please somebody call for help, save me from this night!

Oh Mum is calling me, I think a treat might in the cards, I need to get downstairs. I am off trundling down, yeah a dental stick - my favourite, this is wonderful, nom nom nommmm, lovely stick, chewy and pure delight. It will save me, save me from this night. Well that did not last long, I need more treats. I am going to tell Mum, she is in the kitchen making Dad a drink. Here goes, woof, woof, woof, woof, well she is looking at me, but she is doing this kind of magician hand thing, just turning them backwards and forwards, and she is saying there are no more treats. WHAAATTTT? Are you kidding me, you have got to be kidding me, right, on this horrendous night, which has been made worse by you and Dad traumatising me, and you are giving me the magician's hands? Well you can piss off. I am going to jump up her thigh, that should do it.

Well I tried to jump up on Mum's thigh but misjudged, and as we have tiled flooring, slipped with my front paws and ended up flat on my belly. Mum then thought I had got the message and just walked over me to the lounge with the drink for Dad… Oh wait, hang on a minute, I could've sworn she had something else in her hand, biscuits maybe? I am going to investigate, pppffftttttt, ppppffffftttt, oh jeez that is my best yet, that smells like rotten eggs, good one! I can't help it people, I am stressed out.

Yes I pissing knew it, just look at him sitting there all smug eating chocolate biscuits! You bastards, as if my night isn't bad enough, they are sitting there stuffing biscuits down 'em. Good job Nanny Hammy isn't here, she would soon have them away.

More bangs, this night is just getting worse and worse! I need to get up close to Mum on the sofa. If I nestle in and cover myself with the blanket, that should help. Ooo Mum has turned the TV up, that's helped block out some of the noise, and as it's nice and warm and cosy under this blanket I do feel a little sleepy, in fact I can feel my eyes getting heavy. I am drifting, people, this might just work…

Oh thank you Baby Jesus, it is morning and I made it through the night! Please people no more fireworks, it is "remember, remember the FIFTH of November", not the pissing 4th or 6th or even 7th ok? so enough, let a dog get some peace. I need food, and I need my walk so I can get some of my mojo back.

Well, just got back from my walk. Bumped into Frankfurter again and asked him how his night was, he said he wished the Germans had won the war, then we wouldn't have to celebrate this stupid tradition, and on this occasion I had to agree. Passed Ginger Bastard, I said "I am surprised you haven't locked yourself in a shed again", he hissed at me as he wasn't quite close enough for a swipe. Finally we passed the Pugly club, he looked traumatised as well, so obviously a bad night for everyone, but hopefully that is it for another year. Got Christmas to look forward to now, my favourite time of the year.

Need another snooze, I think, to truly recover from the horrors of last night, but will just check Twitter before I snuggle. Oooo Stuffed Bastard tweeted a pic of herself standing at a bonfire in the back garden, caption "Hot Stuff!" I have got to admit this Stuffington broad is funny.

I think I shall tweet back a pic of me with a sparkler in my paw, saying watch out Stuffington this might ignite you HA, let's see what she makes of that.

Well people, I need to sleep, so

Treats: 0 (a bit early, only just had breakfast)

Birds stared at: 1 (the robin is back, aww)

Pigeon bastards barked at: 1 (on my walk, it decided to strut in front of me, TWAT)

Saturday

Yes alright I have been away for two whole days, I just couldn't be bothered ok? I needed lots of loving and lots of snuggly warm cuddles from Mum, but I am back now people, and whoo hoo, it's only a few weeks until Christmas, "dashing through the snow", la, la, la, la, la! I so hope I get a new toy, usually I do and then after about an hour they end up in the patch! Or bin, like poor Froggy No Eyes, he was fun for about 30 minutes, obviously he wasn't made robust enough for the likes of me, HA, HA! That's the thing with Jack Russell's, we are fierce little bastards, even fat ones like me, so any toy, no matter what it is made of, does NOT beat us people, we will destroy anything you give us. Mum has not yet found an indestructible toy, so that is something for you to think about folks, a toy that does not lose its eyes, stuffing, or squeak in under 30 minutes.

I hear my bungee, so back in a mo, and when I get back I shall check Twitter, and see what Stuffed Bastard has been tweeting.

What a walk this morning, wowzers! Ginger Bastard has a new collar. I shouted "does your head explode now, if you go out of range?" Ha, I swear to god he wanted to scratch my eyes out, calm down Ginge, it's for your own safety. I spotted Ian Beagle, and then Bassett, who looks all doom and gloom every time you see him. His eyes always look sad. I did try and cheer him up, by telling him about Ginger Bastard, but his expression never changed. In fact he reminds me of that cartoon dog, oooo what was his name, Deputy Dawg, that was it, that's him ha, twins. Yes we saw Douglas, I think it's time he got admitted to the mental home up the road, he is off his head, bark, bark, bark, bark. In fact I think his owner is fed up, as today he actually yanked his lead, a bit too hard for my liking as Douglas's eyes bulged a bit… I nearly ran to help him, but running for me is a no go area, and besides it was only a matter of seconds before he looked ok again, and it did shut him up. Seriously though I don't think his owner should yank quite so hard, it's not pleasant. That time Mum did it with me at the bonfire, I thought she had fractured my windpipe, mind you part of that was my fault…

I need to go and check Twitter, but not before breakfast. I hope we are still on sausage pieces, and she hasn't gone and changed it. I don't mind a different variety of treats, but the main meal needs to stay the same. Oh I can smell my favourite, yes, yes, yes, it's sausage pieces, nom nom nommmm! Happy tail wag, can't talk right now, mouth full of glorious moist sausage pieces…

Well, that is interesting, Stuffed Bastard has tweeted a pic of me and her together. How did she do that? I've not sent her any pics of myself… And what is even more interesting people, it has had over 67 likes! Folks must want us to be friends. I like the pic as well, she is just sitting looking forlorn with me lying on my back (not sure about exposing myself like that though!) and I am looking at her, with the caption, "Wanna get stuffed?" Hey that is a bit rude! but hell, in for a penny in for a pound. And if this is what people want, who am I to deprive them? I need to figure out more ways to gain her attention, but for now maybe a little snooze would help.

The snooze fest lasted longer than I anticipated, in fact Mum and Dad have had to wake me from my slumber, and now Nanny Hammy and Granddad Potato are here AGAIN, what's the problem, run out of food in your house have you? I do love my nanny and granddad though, I bet she has some good treats. I am off to see.

Nom nomm nommmmm, what a mouth-watering treat this is, it tastes of turkey and stuffing, and it is shaped in a bone (I know, it's amazing) and it is just so goddam delicious. I don't want it to end, leave me, I am in turkey heaven. Hang on, I can hear music and laughter, OH NO, I think the gin is out again! Last time Mum had that I thought a dragon was living inside of her, it makes her weird. I must go and see…

Yes, people, it's gin, and what's worse is Nanny Hammy is into the martinis, it's not even Christmas yet, what the hell is happening? I can hear Mum saying something, "Happy Anniversary", to Nanny Hammy and Granddad Potato. Anniversary of what? How many years she has spent eating all our food, or how many years spent shouting at Granddad? Well whatever it is they all seem happy. In fact nobody is paying any attention to me whatsoever, this is not on, I will steal that show, then they will all be sorry! I need to fix this, I need to get the limelight back on me, me, me, me, me, me, me - it's all about me.

I have done the most amazing thing people! I stood on one spot at Nanny Hammy's feet, and I pulled off the saddest, cutest look I could muster with my big eyes, and then I reached up with both paws and rested my head on her lap. That broad melted! HA, in your face anniversary, I have stolen the show. Nanny Hammy could not resist, in fact she even thought I had come to wish her a Happy Anniversary as well. Piss off, I ain't bothered about that, now gimme, gimme, gimme another one of them turkey and stuffing sticks.

Well I didn't get another stick, but I did get lots of attention and a big bristly kiss from Nanny. She has more hair on her top lip than Mum, it tickles my face, but I love it. I think they are playing cards now, so will go and have a lie down in my comfy bed with Monkey Boy, who, people, I have decided can stay. He keeps me company and he is warm to snuggle up to when Mum is not available; however, it does mean I need a new item for my patch. I need to get mooching, after this snooze maybe, or tomorrow. Yeah I shall look tomorrow, as it's Sunday.

Sunday

Good morning people, I have slept through and didn't even hear Nanny Hammy and Granddad potato leave, so must have been in a zonked-out coma. Maybe Nanny drugged me with that turkey stick, I shall have to watch that. Anyway, I have been up hours, as for some reason Mum keeps getting up at a ridiculous hour even though it's Sunday, and I have already been on my walk, nothing interesting to report.

But I can say that I have checked my Twitter and I think I am becoming a little obsessed with it all, and it is actually starting to make my paws ache. I am always trying to find new ways to get likes feed my self-absorbed ego!

Ooo I have just had an idea for a pic opportunity for Twitter. Back in a mo…

Now if that doesn't get a lot of likes, I don't know what will! I have posted myself, with a guitar and shades, caption "Hound Dog!" How brilliant am I, you love it people. Hang on I think I can hear Mum shouting bye to Dad, it must be time for his genteel pussy sport of badminton… Talking of which, did I tell you that aside from his other two fitness attempts, he also tried lifting weights? That was another funny story. He bought these dumbbell things from somewhere called the Amazon (I am sure that's a jungle! maybe they were used by strong jungle men). Anyway, they arrived, and he immediately started to use them with gusto. Mum said if he carried on he would end up with guns, I really hoped not as guns are dangerous, people. Granddad used to have a gun and he went shooting clay pigeons with it… I used to cower in the corner when he told us the stories of his shoots, sounded scary to me, in fact any loud noises scare me - oh sorry, I wandered, back to Dad and his weights. Well he used them for about a week, then one day he tried to add extra kilos to them, and he dropped one on his toe!

All I can say is, again, the obscenities were atrocious and Mum was laughing (she really must not like Dad!). He was hopping around shouting, looking very pale, and I was hiding under the table, didn't want to risk anything falling on me. The very next day the weights were put in the garage, never to be seen again. So Dad and his new fitness regimes are a common occurrence. So far he seems to be sticking with this one, maybe because it's for pussies! Who knows, but what I do know is it's time for snuggly wuggly with Mum, so see ya later, alligator…

I am back from the most amazing snooze fest ever! Yes, yes, I say this all the time, but seriously folks snooze time with Mum is the best, as she lets me get in real close to her and strokes my belly, which I love. Anyway, Dad is back now and all three of us are going for a walk, which is quite a rarity as usually it's either Mum takes me or Dad. Sometimes they argue about whose turn it is, they must really love me to fight over who gets to take me, but more often than not it's Mum.

So we are off round the farmer's field. I shall report back later on my return.

That was fun, we bumped into lots of people, but Mum and Dad didn't really stop to chat. I think they are quite anti-social bastards, as no one ever comes to the house, apart from that one time when the smelly mechanic man came, oh and Nanny and Granddad, but that's it. Maybe they don't have any friends, but Dad must have one, who he does badminton with, weird. Anyhow, on the way back, we had to walk on the big main scary road. I don't like this - too many cars go whizzing past. I have to walk on the inside, as sometimes I have a tendency to try and chase the cars, much to Mum's horror! So I am always on a short lead if we ever have to walk this way, which to be fair is almost never, but Dad says I need to toughen up. He's one to talk, pussy! (again, don't let Dad read this) But to be honest, Dad always keeps me safe and sound, so he must love me.

We are finally back home in the warm and I am worn out, my little stumps are aching, must be my Arthur's ritus playing up. Oh that reminds me, when Granddad was here last night, I did hear him complaining a lot about his knees, and how the cold affects them, then Nanny Hammy started moaning. That's when I sloped off to my comfy bed. I thought bloody hell, it's like a piss bag nursing home, I can do without that, next they will be dribbling like me when I beg for food.

Oh before I go…

Treats today: 2 (a grass stick, yum! and a bone biscuit)

Birds stared at: 4 (I could see them in the hedges)

Pigeon bastards barked at: lots and lots, winged rats were hanging out in the farmer's field, that was fun!

Chapter 7 - No Real Christmas Tree for Us

Friday

Hi folks, well I have had a couple of weeks away, not like away, away, at boot camp or that godforsaken kennel place they once sent me to, which I shall tell you people had to be the worst time of my life, worse than bonfire hell! I got abandoned in this place that looked like Folsom Prison (I watched the movie with Mum). I was kept in a giant cage with concrete walls, and all these other dawgies were in similar cages, and the sounds at night were ghastly. I could not understand why Mum and Dad had left me, with NO prior warning, just drove me there and passed me to this butch looking woman, and drove away. I thought I could see Mum doing her ugly crying, but couldn't be sure.

Anyway, the first night I slept on this plastic hard hideous bed. I did have my own blanket, but it made little difference to the cold rough feeling of it. All the other dogs were howling, and rattling the bars with their paws. Next to me was a big scary-looking dog; however, he became my saviour and friend for the time I was there. His name was Bob, and he was a boxer. I shall never forget Bob.

So, I was there for a whole week, and trust me people when I say my anal glands had worked strenuously! By the time Mum and Dad came back to fetch me, I was a huge stinking bag of stress. Mum came in first, and she was so shocked by the sight of me, she actually broke down in ugly crying tears. I was too relieved to feel anything other than delight and pure happiness that they had come back.

All I can say is that I NEVER got sent there again, and Mum and Dad sacrificed what I now know was a holiday to some hot place… I mean why would they want to go somewhere hot anyway? I hate the heat, allergies, sweating, panting, the list goes on, but it's a memory I don't really like recalling, so let's move on, people.

So these last couple of weeks or so I have also taken a break from Twitter and my diary, as I was starting to disconnect with real life, and there was nothing really to report. Same old, same old, lots of sleeping, eating, and farting, no newbies on my walk, Frankfurter has a new coat, it's some tartan creation (why do you humans love tartan!). Oh talking of coats, I have a funny Christmas story, I shall regale you with it later, but for now I am back with a vengeance and guess what people, it's DECEMBER, which means it will be Christmas in 4 weeks! It's time for the countdown, "deck the halls with bones and biscuits, fa, la, la, la, la, la, la, la, la, everyone bring me dental sticks, fa, la, la, la, la, la, la, la, la."

Yipppeeeeee, I am going to check Twitter! Well, well, well, Stuffington has obviously missed me, because there are over 15 tweets from her, some saying she is worried that I have been neglected, and some just of cute pics of her. I need to tweet back and tell her I am safe, but before I do, I can hear Dad is back from shopping, so I am gonna take my udders and ass to the kitchen and see what delights he has.

Nommm nomm nommmm, you are not gonna, nom nomm, believe this, nom nom, but I have got the biggest, nom nom, the bestest, nom, and the tastiest bone evvveeerrrrr! It has something called marrow in the middle, nom nom nom, and my tongue is snaking in and out, nom nom, of this bad boy, in fact it's starting to ache… I can't quite reach fully in, nom nommm nommm, I have to go. This needs my complete and utter full attention. Back soon.

Ppppfffffftttt, pppppffffttttt, ooops, it has to be the marrowbone… OH JESUS, that smells like the drains, I have to escape myself! I shall waddle back to the kitchen, well Dad is still putting the shopping away, so where is Mum? I need to find her, I have to get outside, ppppffffttttt, like now, where the hell is she, whining noises now, ppppfffft, oh god this is bad! Oh I hear her she is coming, come on, come on, come on, I need to go out, OPEN THE DOOR, phew I am out. Ppppffffttt, evacuation people - I am NEVER eating marrowbone again, that has gone straight through me. For the love of god, what did they put in that? I mean it lured me in, it tasted so divine, but Christ, that has not done my insides any good. It is Dad's fault, in fact I can hear Mum shouting at him, "Why on earth did you buy him that shit? He's exploded all over the garden!" Erm excuse me I have not exploded, I am still in one piece. Oh dear Mum is now outside hosing! It was bad, looked like watery brown gravy, but did not smell like gravy!

Talking of gravy, I hope we get that really yummy stuff with BEEF this Christmas, and not like last year, with a stupid Turkey Crown, I mean WTF a turkey who wears a crown? How absurd. Also I need to mention the lack of a real Christmas tree, we are not allowed, well I say we, *I* am not allowed a real one. It was some years ago now and I was still young and naïve, and Mum had purchased this bloody great big real fir tree.

I can still remember the horror, and those goddam needles… I kept finding those spiky bastards for weeks after, and every so often one would get stuck in my paw, now people that is like torture. Anyway back to the tree, Mum dragged it in, Dad was nowhere to be seen… In fact I think Mum bought it without Dad knowing, as I know what he would've said, "bloody great stupid expense for one ffing day" (bah humbug, he is a tight arse), and there was Mum all proud, and starry-eyed, decorating this thing. The Christmas music was on, if I recall - the one song I remember was by Boney M, because all I could conjure up was a juicy bone, and she was also drinking GIN, yeah people that's right my Mum is a gin fiend.

So, this tree was being decorated to the hilt, and Mum was swaying, and not to the music, Ha!

Then the lights came out, she was getting rather angry, as they seemed to be twisted like a snake (arrgggh black snake, flashback!!), but eventually she managed to untangle them and wrap them round this monstrous tree, which to me looked a bit cockeyed, it was like leaning to one side. I thought, maybe it's had some gin too! Then came the big reveal, WHATEVER! She stood back all smug and switched the lights on, and this tree looked all sparkly and in fact quite mesmerising, I was a little hypnotised by it.

I suddenly realised then, that this was a tree, and I love, love, love trees! I like to sniff them, and dance round them, and then I love to cock my little stumpy leg up them and relieve myself, this is pure pleasure. So of course I thought, here was my very own weeing tree, what a wonderful, thoughtful, Christmas gift! Well Mum left the room, rather wobbly I thought, and I think went upstairs, maybe for a lie down, but by this point I did not care. I ran over to that tree and starting sniffing it and circling it and doing my best jiggly tree dance, and just as I was about to cock my stump, disaster people! It was like in slow motion, this monstrous tree, which was already leaning to one side, started to fall and it was aiming right for me! I couldn't get out from under it fast enough, and then crash, that bastard fell right on top of me, there were baubles everywhere, the lights went out, and I had sparkly string stuff in my mouth. I started to bark as loud as I could, but Mum was nowhere to be seen. I thought this is odd, normally her hearing is like a bat's, and she can hear when I have been up to no good, but no - nothing, nada, zilch.

Then, like a miracle sent by the baby Jesus, in walks Dad, and he runs over to the tree, shouting and swearing and saying "WTF is this?" and "oh come on my boy are you hurt?" and "where's your Mum?" Well how the f**k do I know stupid, I have been trapped under this monster! So Dad starts looking for Mum and he found her upstairs, ASLEEP on the bed, a-pissing-sleep people! Talk about serious neglect, I could've died, then what? But my Dad, he saved me.

Anyway the tree got put back to its correct position, but Dad wasn't happy, and said that it was being taken down the day after Christmas and we would never have a real tree again, in fact we might not have any tree, as he said they are cheap and shitty-looking things. (Miserable fart!) Oops sorry I mean that's right Dad, that tree could've been the end of me.

So we do not have a real tree for Christmas, people, but what we do get is lots of presents, and some of the ones I have received over the years, you would split your sides at. In fact I will now tell you the tale of the coat! Mum thought that as I was getting older (and fatter!), I needed to keep warm in the winter. Dad disagreed and said I already had a bloody fur one, but he lost that argument, again! so the coat story.

A couple of Christmases ago, it was very cold indeed, and there was this wondrous white stuff on the floor. I now know it's called snow, and the joy of this fluffy stuff was heaven for me. Not so for Mum who hated the stuff, and in fact misunderstood my wheezing asthmatic breathing that I sometimes do, and thought I was freezing, but NO, people - when I laugh too hard, it sometimes causes me to catch my breath and then I wheeze, it's highly amusing… Anyway, because of this Mum decided I needed a coat to keep me warm.

So Christmas morning came round, and I was very excited. I love it, the music, the smells, the atmosphere, it is marvellous! Mum and Dad start giving each other gifts, usually Dad's gifts to Mum are brilliant, yet Mum's are normally shit, and have to go back in the new year, ha ha ha. In fact one year I heard Dad ask for an OMD music CD, and when he opened it, it was ELO! Talk about awkward! How can you get those letters mixed up? Even I couldn't get that wrong, and my spelling and understanding of words is dreadful. So anyhow, it was time for my pressie, and I was like, gimme, gimme, gimme, hoping and praying it was a new toy as good as the Froggy No Eyes that I had one year (RIP Froggy)… Mum had to help me, I can only tear with my teeth, and the sticky stuff on it gets all in my mouth, pah, yuk, so there she is helping me rip the paper off, and I could see fur… I thought yippeee, and then I could see it was like a light tan colour, so I am thinking, ooo a bear, perhaps a cat, wow even better, I can pretend it's Ginger Bastard, but then it fully appeared.

People, I cannot even begin to describe the a) horror, b) disappointment and c) like WTF? There lying on the floor was some kind of coat (not tartan thank god), but in fact this was worse - it looked like something Del Boy used to wear in the 80's classic Only Fools and Horses. It was made from sheepskin, uuurrrghhhh! For starters, who wants to wear a dead sheep's skin? and secondly, it had fur around the neck and on the inside.

I tell you, I thought, I am not pissing wearing that! I tried to grab it in my mouth and shake it to see if it was still alive. Mum took this as meaning I liked it, and started cooing all gooey eyed at Dad, "Oh see he loves it", and "let's try it on him". Errrr NO let's pissing not.

Yes people, the inevitable happened - Mum grabbed hold of me and tried to force this hideous dead thing on me, but HA, HA, HA, in your face, it didn't fit! and I can tell you now folks, this was one time when I was glad of my mother freaking udders, the bloody thing wouldn't zip up round my belly, and I was sooooo happy, in fact it started another wheezing asthma attack, I was laughing so much. Dad said, "look it's stressed him out" and "take it bloody off him, stupid idea, anyway". I was like yeah you should listen to Dad more often, now get this bastard off me.

So folks, I only get toys for Christmas now, and sometimes the odd treat, but have to be careful with them, especially after the unfortunate marrowbone incident… Anyway I need to check Twitter, and go for a walk methinks, then snooze time.

Twitter has gone mental, apparently some advert has been "dropped", whatever that means (sounds like it could've hurt itself), and everyone is talking about it, so of course I tweeted Stuffed Bastard and asked what all the fuss was about.

She explained it's a big Christmas thing every year, with someone called John Lewis, and he makes a heart-warming advert using animals. I was like super excited and said we should audition and maybe we could star in one, me and Stuffington, her on my back as I trot (waddle) through fields of snow, carrying her to a big sparkly tree, and then I drop her and piss up it. Brilliant! How many views would that bad boy get? I am a genius, I need to get this actioned, but for now I need a walk, and I can hear the bungee…

Well, have just got back from my walk, with Mum, and obviously I had to relieve myself, and depending on which orifice it comes out of, Mum has to clean up after me, and so carries these little bag things around with her. I sometimes hear her complaining though that she finds them in every bloody coat pocket she owns! Anyway, something very odd happened, I thought I had fully evacuated and so was happily trundling back with Mum, when bam! my arsehole needed to empty for a third time. People, I was like WTF, but had to stoop right where I was, and it wasn't the greatest of places, it was in fact in the middle of the road.

I was mortified and terrified all at the same time, firstly I could not explain this third expulsion, and secondly what if a car came speeding round the bend and ploughed into me? I mean Mum could've at least jumped out the way, me I was stuck like a rabbit in the headlights squatting for all I was worth, looking rather alarmed.

That was not the worst of it though, as Mum had used all the pooh bags… Even though she is always complaining that they pop up in every goddam pocket, not so on this occasion! No, she had to somehow figure out how to pick up my dainty but somewhat smelly deposit without having a new bag.

Ingeniously, she decided to use an already full bag, and carefully managed to scoop in the newcomer. I was seriously impressed, it was like watching an episode of the Krypton Factor, that great 80's show, where contestants had to solve puzzles, that was until I heard her swearing, and realised she didn't quite manage it and had my stinking shit on her fingers, ha ha ha ha ha! It's just reminded me of a joke: "What's green and smells like pork?" "Kermit's finger" Too much? I think it's funny.

So Mum is seriously not happy, mumbling to herself, saying there's shit everywhere, me I am at least over the trauma of Poohgate and am happily bumbling along next to her. She seems to have quickened her pace and my little stumps are working overtime, whoa slow down, oh thank god I can see our house… Mum is still muttering and, oh Jesus what is that smell, why is she putting her shitty fingers near my face? I have no desire to smell them thank you, oh she's taking my bungee off, in I go. Time for me to check Twitter. Mum has gone to wash her hands, thank god. I don't want my food served with them and stinking of shit.

I've had my afternoon snack, as not only do I get breakfast, I also get a small snack in the afternoon (yes I hear you saying, maybe that's why he's fat), well it's not just that entirely, ok? I am off for a nap, but when I return I shall explain why I am a fat bastard.

Treats today: 4 (Dad kept sneaking them to me)

Birds stared at: 3 (I think it's getting too cold now)

Pigeon Bastards barked at: 0

P.S. I don't think it will be worth reporting on the birds through winter as I don't see a lot now… it's dark most mornings, it's dark in the afternoons, and in between I just can't be bothered. Too goddam cold.

Saturday

Ha Ha, yes I slept through again, it's this bloody clock thing, messed up my biorhythms, and also when it is dark out I have nothing to stare at except my reflection, and although I am one handsome dude, I can only stare at myself for so long. So I sleep, the fire gets put on and I snuggle up to Mum or Dad, mostly Mum, and drift off, but don't you judge me. Anyway, it is now only 3 weeks until Christmas and Mum is getting excited, Dad is moaning about cost (whoever he is), and me I am super happy, arrrrgghhhhhhh well I was - I can hear black snake, and not the music, people. Oh god why he is out again? He comes out at least once a week, I don't mention it because it's too traumatising… I always have to go and bark at him, so needs must and all that. I shall be back soon when I have conquered the black snake…

Well, that went well, NOT. Mum did her usual thing of pushing him at me, I am sure she is a sadist (I have said it before) and I was barking at him and trying to bite him, but he is a ferocious little bastard. He makes this weird noise, and the bloody great snake thing on him, uuurrggghh! But he has gone back in his hidey hole for now, so drama over folks. After my walk I shall regale you all with the story of why I am fat, then you will all be like ooo we are sorry Rupert, oooo we shouldn't have judged you.

Back from my walk. Ginger Bastard was nowhere to be seen, I hope he hasn't gone and got locked in a shed again, or worse, his head has actually exploded - what a mess that would make HA. I saw Frankfurter, and he was happily waddling along in his tartan coat, looks like a bit of a dick to me! (For real! Ha Ha.) Spotted Pugly Club, and his Dad was wearing some hideous Christmas jumper, with, get this, a picture of Pugly on it. I thought, it's bad enough seeing the two of them in real life, let alone now on a jumper, truly repugnant. The only place that jumper should be is in my serial killer patch, which I haven't been to for a while, but the ground is too hard, so probably won't get to go out to it until the spring, but I digress, sorry. We also passed Douglas, we crossed the road before he spotted us, so didn't have to endure his possessed barking, he's a dickhead too. And that was it this morning, now time for my tale.

When I was a young man, and in my prime, Mum and Dad decided to do the most gruesome and most shocking thing that they could do to a dawgie like me! They wrapped me in the special blanket (at this point I didn't know it was going to be a special blanket), and off we went on a journey. I was sitting up front on Mum's knees - it was a bit wobbly, so I had to keep popping my head out the window, now that was fun, whooo reading hoooooo! Anyway, we arrived at what I thought was another house, and we all got out of the car and walked to this house, but my spidey senses were on high alert and I could smell strange smells, something medical, and other dogs' anal glands… I panicked and started heading back down the driveway, but Mum wasn't having any of it, and picked me up, but she didn't just hold me normal, NO, and people let me tell you NO DOG likes this, she held me like a baby, that is the worst thing you can do to a dawgie. We do not like being tipped on our backs, unless we are safely on the floor and it's us in control, OK, so there I was on my back in this goddam blanket and I was wriggling and whining, Mum was trying to soothe me, Dad was trying to be manly, and in we walked.

The smells got stronger and by this time I had added my own smell, with my stress glands operating at full pelt. I was panting and glassyeyed. I heard a man say, "aww here's the fella", "let's get him out back" and "you can come and fetch him after 3pm later today, should be all done by then".

My mind was in overdrive. What was out back, why were they leaving me, WTF was happening? It was traumatic people T.R.A.U.M.A.T.I.C.…

Before I continue, I need to tell you that any human who does this to a dog wants tying down in a field and being smeared in honey, with ants poured over them, yes that is how bad it is.

So I was taken out back and hooked up to some kind of small snake thing, and all of a sudden I can feel myself floating and my eyes, they will not stay open. For the love of god, I thought, what is this, I'm being drugged and they are going to use me in some freak circus show… Then NOTHING, blackness, can't even tell you a thing people, I was out of it.

When I came back to reality, it was ghastly. I thought, who the hell has put a plastic lampshade on my head? does this amuse you, am I funny to you? Ha. And that is when I discovered, to my horror, that my pride and joy, my weeing machine, my love dangle was as limp and as a floppy as a week old lettuce, and why? Because my massive NUT SACK had been removed! This was apparently for my own health, and to prevent later disease in life… But they were MY nuts, mine! And it was my decision to say if you could chop them off. What kind of barbaric world are we living in?

Well, that was it, if Mum or Dad (the bastard who still has his) thought I was going to talk to them anymore, they could piss off, and in fact when they came back to fetch me, I completely and utterly froze them out. I somehow managed to turn my head away in disgust with this goddam contraption on it, and what was even better was Mum couldn't get in to kiss me, that is how big that bastard was. I couldn't walk straight either, so had to be carried, the indignity was horrendous and I could feel a phantom twinge where my nuts were, to make matters worse.

When we got home, they laid me on this bed they had made up in the lounge, which I must admit was comfy, but to my horror I couldn't even lay my head down, because of the lampshade. Mum decided after an hour to take it off, which I was grateful for, and of course my first reaction was to lick my impressive nut sack, but to my dismay I realised again that they weren't there anymore and it was the phantom twinge I felt. What a cruel, cruel world you live in people.

I started to lick the stitches, but then this evoked a shout from Mum. I thought you can piss off, you have NO right to shout at me, I will lick what the hell I want and when I want, but again true to form, Mum was right as I only managed to make the area sore, so gave up that fight after 20 minutes.

I was so distressed by the whole event that I fell into a deep restful sleep, I think I heard Mum say it was Anne's prosthetic or something like that (yeah get me some false nuts)… Anyway, I had to face facts, and soon got used to not having them bad boys swinging around my rear end. To be fair having them off was a blessing in disguise, as not only did it mean I wouldn't get a disease, it also meant I wouldn't be haunted by ladies' smells, as that would've driven me insane, so I had to man up and I did eventually give Mum a super Rupert cuddle, I shall tell you about those later.

So the reason, people, as to why I am now fat, is when you remove a dawgie's nuts, he loses something manly, and this in turn slows things down, so I struggle now with burning the calories, and before you go say anything about how I should eat less, PISS OFF, ok? I am a) old, b) it's none of your goddam business, and c) mind your beeswax ok, so up yours HA.

All this regaling has made me sleepy, so I need a little snooze, and as it's Saturday, both Mum and Dad should be on the sofa, I am off to see… YES they are snuggled together under a blanket - I am going to get in the middle of them like I do at night night time… oooo heaven, be back soon.

I am back and that was some nap, it's gone dark again, it does that now, gets dark really quickly. I have checked Twitter and excitement is mounting for Christmas; everyone is trying to tweet the cutest pic. Of course I tweeted one, already it has had 49 likes. I was dressed as an elf and added the caption, "We shall get by with a little "elf" from your friend" - ha ha ha, I told you I am the next Michael McIntyre…

I also have 105 followers now, which is crazy considering I am just a mere dawgie, but people like what they like. I tweeted Stuffed Bastard and asked what she was doing for Christmas, but she said it wasn't her favourite time of the year, as it was when her "Dad" got stuck in an elevator and died. He was apparently the doorstop for some posh hotel and his job was to hold the elevator doors open, until one day, he got kicked inside of it and couldn't reach the buttons to open the doors himself, so he died of dehydration. How awful, I said, but not to worry, I would keep her company over the festive season with regular tweets. She liked that I think.

Well, it's time for another lie down methinks, and besides, Mum and Dad will be watching this brilliant show with my other fave David Attenborough, he makes A.M.A.Z.I.N.G. shows. The one from last week was breathtaking, it had penguins on it, and there were like thousands of them, I couldn't stop barking at the TV, it was great. I am going to see if it's on later and so might just have to stay awake, also I think Nanny Hammy and Granddad potato might be gracing us with their presence. I hope so, I like presents, lots of them please.

I was right, Nanny and Granddad have turned up, and I was laughing so much, I nearly choked on the treat Nanny gave me. They looked like the Chuckle Brothers tonight, dressed in similar outfits. I thought, what is it about you oldies, when you get past your prime, you lose all your dress sense and end up wearing similar costumes! Tonight they were both in navy, and even Mum laughed and said "twins", except they are not identical, no way.
Like I say, Granddad looks like a potato, and Nanny looks like a hamster with all puffed out cheeks and chins (not for Nanny's eyes!). Also, why do they lose their sense of rhythm? I know this because the other week, when they were here again gorging on our food, the music was on in the background and it was Dad's favourite 80's, and in strolls Nanny and starts jigging from side to side. She looked like a giant space invader. I turned tail, as if I had carried on staring in morbid fascination I would've surely had a wheezing attack. Obviously getting older has no benefits. I mean look at me, I have this Arthur's ritus to contend with like Granddad, and swinging udders. It's a torturous world folks we live in.

So back to tonight, they are participating in some game or other and Nanny has a glass of martini and Granddad has what I can only describe as a glass of piss, and it can't be having a very good effect on him either as Nanny is shouting "Oo Arthur, you can only have one, how are you going to drive us home else?" so it must be potent stuff. Yuk, I hate the smell of booze, so much so, I don't even go in for kisses much when Mum has been on the gin, she stinks something awful. Dad, well he hardly drinks these days, as apparently he can't hold his licker any more. Ooo I have a licker, it's called my tongue and I can hold mine, like I say Dad is a pussy… oooh I meant to tell you about my special loves I give with my tongue.

So when I am feeling especially loving, I like to clamber on Mum when she is lying on the sofa, and I get up real close to her face. I then place my giant paws on either side of her face and hold her in place with my claws, she doesn't like this bit much, then I shove my enormous long tongue right up her nose! Yummy, yummy, yummy, you humans must have a salt bath up there or something because boy does it taste good, and once I've licked I just can't stop, so I keep trying to snake my tongue in and out, much to Mum's utter revulsion. She starts yelling "gerroff Rupert", but it's like a drug and that is why, being the superior one I am, I grip her face with my paws, as it pins her down, HA super genius. So my extra special loving, people, is my secret obsession of nose licking. I just loves me a bit of nose.

Well I can hear Nanny Hammy and Granddad potato are going, so it must be time for David Attenborough and snuggle times with Mum and Dad, so I am off to say bye, and then have me a right old bark at the TV…

Sunday

Alright, I fell asleep again and have slept through, so what, but last night was exhausting. I managed to stay awake for David Attenborough, and it had these crabs on and there were like thousands and thousands and I just could not stop barking at them. Mum and Dad thought it was hilarious, and kept egging me on, saying things like "aww what's that Rupert, are they in the lounge?" I have said a million times I am not the idiot here people, how can they be in the lounge, but I go along with it, as it amuses them. Anyway, these crabs were hypnotic and they all crawl sideways, which was fascinating. I tried copying them but stumbled on my stumps and fell over. Then I decided I could wriggle round and round on my side and this then became more fun, so much so I went dizzy and then had to be helped onto the sofa.

It was at this point I did drift into a deep slumber snuggled up cosy, and apparently I snored very loudly… Mum videoed me and so I have put this on Twitter, everyone loved it, in fact it has had over 30 retweets, and 60 likes, so methinks more videos are the way.

Dad I can hear is NOT going to badminton. HA, I knew it wouldn't last long, this "new" fitness regime, pussy, what is it this time? Well he has injured his knee and has some fluid on it… Any excuse, if you ask me, but he apparently needs to rest it, so he will be here all day, messing with my snuggle plans, bastard.

Oh I might as well tell you the only other fitness attempt he tried and that was cycling. He bought a bike, and all the gear, and again I couldn't stop laughing when he came downstairs, the one day. I heard Mum say, "Dear GOD, you cannot go out dressed in those, you will be arrested!" I think she was referring to his still intact NUTS (again, bastard!) which were protruding from the shorts, so I trundled in to have a look, and had a wheezing attack, such was the shock of it.

It looked like he had two baby rats fighting to get out of his underpants, and I nearly attacked them, in fact I had to get up and have a sniff, so I jumped up (when I could still jump) and pushed my nose right in there. Dad shouted "Get down Rupert", Mum was laughing harder, and of course Dad was NOT amused, ooooooo! He also had on this ridiculous-looking hat, which didn't suit his potato head at all, and it had a straplike thing that went under his chin, which just enhanced the potato look!

But he was determined (again) to get fit, so off he went for his first ride. People I tell you now, this is the gospel according to Rupert, he managed only to go round the block, which I could walk back in those days in under 15 minutes, so on a bike, I imagine it would take less than 5. I was in pieces. Mum was stood at the door, and I heard her say, "well done, but you're no Chris Hoy yet, are you?" Oh he didn't like that, in fact he doesn't like my Mum's humour one bit, I think she is side-splitting and maybe that is where I get it from!

So the bike and all the gear went in the garage, and I think got sold, who knows? It could still be there, but I can't tell, as there is so much crap in there, you could start your own bring and buy sale.

Well, all this storytelling has made me hungry… I am going to see what pleasures are cooking in the kitchen, sometimes on a Sunday, Mum cooks sausages, and bacon, and egg, nom nom nommm…

Yipppeeeeeee, I am delirious people, Mum is cooking a breakfast, maybe to cheer pussy Dad up, who knows, who cares… all I know is I can smell bacon and sausage, and it is glorious. I have to get my begging face on, so I am off to practice in the patio doors. I can still just see my reflection, as it's grey and dreary this morning. Back soon…

I am the master, all bow down to me, that was brilliant, I am B.R.I.L.L.I.A.N.T. I got to the table where Mum and Dad sometimes sit together all civil like (not very often, Ha), and I waddled up to Dad first, to chance my luck with him. I sat close to his leg and rested my head on his foot, then I looked up at him with my eyes, and I know from that angle when you look down, my eyes look HUGE, and soulful and sad… It worked, people, I could hear Dad say, "oh my boy, you after some bacon, or what about a bit of sausage?" I was like, "don't ask such a dumb pissing question, just gimme!" and then it happened, Dad had cut up a bit of sausage and bacon on his plate, and he let me eat it from the plate, just like a human. I was in seventh heaven, my tongue made sure I licked every single inch of that plate, and boy was it good. I can hear judging, people, well you can all piss right off OK? The plate gets washed, I am not contaminated, and yeah, yeah, I am fat. I told you the diet malarkey days are long behind me.

I can hear Mum shouting "walkies", so I have to go and see what delights are out and about this morning… Dad is obviously in some kind of bacon coma, as he is now resting on the sofa. He can just budge over when I get back, that is mine and Mum's place, on a Sunday.

Back from the walk, and boy did I laugh, Ginger Bastard is still alive and well, and was obviously in a foul mood. When I shouted to him, "what's it like to be kept prisoner?", he hissed something terrible, and said the reason I hadn't seen him was because he now relieves himself in the house, in a tray! and was being kept in a lot more. I said, "WTF, who shits in their house, you dirty bastard, what kind of freak weirdo are you? That is so disgusting". He told me it was ok because he did it over some gravel type stuff, and it absorbs it, still I don't care what you say people, that is so unhygienic shitting in the house. What is the world coming to? I don't think I can look at Ginger Bastard in the same way ever again.

Moving on, we passed Ian Beagle, and Bassett, still looking as sad as ever even though it's nearly Christmas, and then I spotted Pomerbitch, and she had on this absurd-looking pink sparkly coat. I couldn't resist shouting, "you can't make a silk purse out of a sow's ear!" Ha Ha Ha, oh the yapping could be heard 50 miles away! We also spotted Frankfurter (Klaus), but he was too busy sniffing the air with his nose, made him look like a right snooty bastard, and that was it. No Douglas, which was very odd, I hope the dumb bastard is ok.

So back home, and Dad is still in the same position, Mum is shouting at him, "Oh thank you for washing up, you lazy bastard!" Well if he washed up, why is she angry? I don't understand, but as Mum now has to go and do some womanly duties, I think I will lie with Dad then, I can get in real close and have a snooze fest.

PPPffffttttttt, that was NOT ME, in fact I have jumped out of my fur, it was that loud. WTF? Oh it was Dad, he is laughing, he thinks he is funny, he is not, that is disgusting. If he doesn't stop I don't think I want to lie with him, even Mum heard it from the kitchen and is shouting, "dirty bugger!".

.

I am definitely getting sleepy, I will just snuggle that little bit closer to Dad, ooooo Mum is here now too, I shall lie here between them for 10 minutes, and dream of Christmas Day, which is nearly here… bliss…

Chapter 8 - Squirrels, Dwarves and Presents

Diary,

I am king of snoozes, it's Sunday evening and I slept all afternoon… In fact I was so comatose, I hadn't noticed that Mum and Dad had moved off the sofa, but now I know I will just stretch myself out and ease myself up gently… Awwwww I smell food, I need to investigate, but first a quick check of Twitter.

I have just tweeted a pic of myself, mid-yawn, but it looks like I am singing, so I added the caption, "on the fifth day of Christmas my Mummy said to me, come here Rupert I think I spot a flea"… Euurrggh fleas! Flashback…

It was when I was very, very young, a pup in fact, and I could feel these things crawling all over through my fur. I tell you people I thought I was going to go insane! What was worse, they were sucking the life force out of me, little hijacking bastard shit bags, horrible offensive jumping feckers, you don't want those, people, us dawgies hate 'em.

Anyway, Mum soon sorted them bastards out. She sprayed me with a special spray, which nearly choked me, but did in fact actually kill em- I could see them jumping off the fur ship, my back! and all dying. It was heaven when I was finally free of them, and now I get treated every so often, to prevent them hijackers from ever hitching a lift on my back again.

So back to food, I need to waddle to the kitchen and see what tantalising delights Mum has in store for moi… Well, I am pretty sure I can smell roast chicken people, my senses are in overdrive, yes, yes, it is, people, she better have saved me some! I just love me a bit of the roast bird, gimme, gimme, gimme! I am standing to attention, I am doing the sad eye look, oooo she's turning, she has spotted me, WHAAAT, WAIT, she is just putting it in the fridge! NOOOOO, why are you doing that??

I am seriously depressed, Mum said I couldn't have the roast chicken tonight as it was too late, and I had already eaten my snack. I was like, well who are you to decide when I am full? I AM NEVER FULL, you dumb broad, oh sorry Mum, but no, I am to wait until the morning when I can have a little for breakfast. I have to now wait a whole 12 hours, before I can feast on that roast chicken. Pah, this is cruelty and warrants me calling that show, someone gimme the number will you, for crying out loud. I have been saying for ages now I need to call. I am going for a lie down as nobody cares, nobody is interested and you are all bastards.

Treats today: 2, maybe 3 (I don't recall)

Monday

I went to bed last night, and to teach them bastards a lesson for withholding the chicken, I slept at the top of the bed in between their pillows, and I made sure I stretched myself out. I even kept prodding my Mum in the back with my paws. Ha, she woke up and was mumbling to Dad how she didn't have a very good night's sleep. Well, let that be a lesson to you.

Now GIVE ME THE CHICKEN. Ooooooo Mum is off to the kitchen. Dad is too, as if I give a rat's ass where Dad is. I am only interested in one thing people and so I am following the traitor, to see if she can redeem herself.

Nommmmmmmmmmmm nommmmmmm nommmmmm, I cannot communicate right now, I am in roast chicken heaven, nom nom nommmmm nommmmmm, oh it's so juicy, lovely, lovely tasty chicken, Mum you are the best, and forgiven - for now.

That was super chicktastic! I can now hear the door, I think Nanny Hammy is here, but in your face Nanny, no chicken left for you to gorge on, no siree, so off you go back home... Oh wait no, she might have a good treat. I am going to greet her with my happiest dance ever, see you in a mo...

That dance had some of the finest moves of all time, I even managed a little twirl today, and it worked because Nanny Hammy produced such an interesting little treat today I was mesmerised for a second. It was bone-shaped, but guess what, it had dry chicken wrapped around it (seriously how does this happen?). What a double whammy bonus of a treat, a small bone with chicken. It was scrumptious, Nanny Hammy is now the best.

Yeah, yeah I am fickle, who cares, I get what I want, and nobody gets hurt in the process, Capiche? So we are off to a new park today. It's an odd feeling, as I like routine, but also I am a little excited at the prospect of new smells... I can hear no-fun bungee, will report back later folks.

Whoooooo hoooooo, I have had the best morning ever, like EVER! We did walk to this park (and so passed the usual one, but I can't be bothered to go into all that now, let's just say, boorrring), and this new park, it had so many trees, I couldn't contain my excitement. I had a wheezy attack, Mum thought I was stressed and needed to go home, but Nanny Hammy said "no, he will be alright".

Nanny Hammy you saved the day, and thank the lord, as amongst the trees, there were… wait for it… wait…

SQUIRREL BASTARDS!! Yes you heard me, these are like vermin with bushy tails, and they think they are cute, but these feckers leap around all squirrelly-like, going crazy with their nuts (not their actual nuts! The eating kind, as they are storing them up for the winter). And let me tell you folks, they are so much fun just to watch, but my squeak went into overdrive.

I so wanted to catch me one of them squirrel bastards! Imagine the fun if I got to keep it hostage, I could taunt it for hours, days, weeks even… I would shake it a bit to quieten it down, then I would just sit on it for a bit looking manic-eyed at it. OMG I tried so hard, I ran, yes people I RAN (I do not know where this newfound energy came from) from tree to tree; Mum was trying to follow and get me reined in.

But I was like, PISS OFF! Nanny Hammy was shouting, I also told her to shut your mouth broad... Then I nearly got one, but disaster! I got the bungee tangled round the tree and nearly choked myself. Mum said it served me right. The squirrel bastard had stopped to look down on me from his branch, I swear to god he gave me the finger, with his tiny little squirrel hands, and Nanny Hammy was saying I think that's enough for one morning, he is a lunatic.

So that was the day, and it was fantastic. I hope we go to that park again, I need a squirrel bastard in my life. Also I need to tweet this, so back in a short while...

I am back, I have tweeted the hell out of that. Stuffed Bastard wanted to know what colour the squirrel was. I was like, who gives a shit, it's a squirrel bastard, why, are you related? HA, but apparently if it's a red squirrel they are on a danger list. Well I said it was very dangerous, kept trying to taunt me, so no wonder.

Nanny Hammy is in the lounge, and she has stuffed I don't know how many biscuits in her gob, maybe she is storing them up for winter HA! No wonder Dad has to go out for shopping every week, it's because Nanny Hammy keeps coming round and stealing our food. Well I think it's about time she went home now. I need a nap and to lie with Mum.

I can hear Mum still talking to Nanny, something about Christmas Day, well what about it? I get up, you treat me like a king, give me food, give me presents and then we sleep all day, so what is there to discuss? But they are discussing what time to cook the lunch, which is going to be some bastard turkey in a crown, crap. Well it better be moist, and not like one year it got overcooked and was so dry, I thought I was eating the stuffing out of Monkey Boy. I had to drink a gallon of water, which then only enhanced my udders - my belly ballooned and I looked like a walking weeble, HA.

Well I think Nanny is going now, and Christmas Day lunch has been arranged, they are going to arrive at 2 p.m., as if I give a shit. However, if they turn up with presents, then fine, I might feign interest, ok. Anyway it's not long now for me to wait, as Christmas Day will be here in less than 2 weeks now, yippeeeee!

Treats today: 1 from Nanny

No birds No Pigeon bastards

Wednesday

How the hell did it get to Wednesday, I don't even recall Tuesday! OMG I must have slept through, seriously these bloody dark nights and mornings are wreaking havoc with my body clock. Oh well, a day closer to the Fat Bastard making an appearance… Call ME greedy, that fecker gets to eat I don't know how many mince pies and nobody judges him, no, it's all right for that fat bastard to shove in whatever he likes.

Well, I have checked Twitter, and there are too many people now dressed as elves, seriously, get your own ideas. What's worse though: some are dressed as dwarves! What is it with them little people? I mean this time of the year, they are everywhere, and always hanging out in sevens… I don't get it, what an odd number. And when they see me, they think because they are low to the ground like me, I will automatically have something in common with them, and so they start to stroke me… Piss off touching me with your tiny little hands, it freaks me out! Yes I know they are adults, but their hands are like them begging munters' hands, and so I always want to bite 'em, like tiny chipolata sausages, nom nom nommmm.

One year, and it wasn't even Christmas, we came across a dwarf couple, I know weird right, out in pairs, and anyway, as we walked by, the male decided to come and say hello. I was already on high alert, thinking what is this giant man-child doing approaching me, gerroff, so I started to growl and Mum shouted at me. Anyway he started stroking my rear end and I was like WTF do not stroke there, and don't even touch my face! "You wanna piece of me?" Ha.

Well, I couldn't take it anymore, so I jumped up him and, with all my weight, I shoved that dwarf bastard on his arse, and then I climbed onto his chest and rammed my tongue up his tiny little nose! That had him, his little arms and legs were flailing around. The female one came running over, well I say running - she looked like me when I try to run, more of a waddle. I was in hysterics, and so started wheezing while still pinning the dwarf down. Mum was mortified, and soon pulled me off and was all like "oh I am so sorry!" To be fair to them both, they did see the funny side and actually walked off laughing. I think I heard them singing Hi Ho, or something, but couldn't swear to it.

Well people, nothing much is happening, have been on my walk… Ginger Bastard is still wearing his stupid collar. I said, "what are you doing out, have you shit the house out, dirty bastard?" He tried clawing at me, but missed. "Ha, watch out", I shouted, "too many sheds for you to get stuck in over Christmas, if you ain't careful!" Didn't see Frankfurter, or even Ian Beagle, but spotted Douglas , and off he went, bark, bark, bark. I shouted, "And a Merry Christmas to you too, you dumb shit!

So back home, and have decided to lie in my comfy bed for a while with Monkey Boy. Mum is upstairs,

I think she is doing her womanly duties, and of course Dad is out doing his man job. I will just have a little nap, then see what gives later.

WTF, I have been awoken from my slumber. I can hear the door, I knew it, it's more parcels for him next door. He is obviously having all the stupid, ugly presents he has ordered delivered. Why don't you get a PO Box mate? Then we wouldn't have to accept them. I wonder what he has ordered now. The other month, we took in a parcel and it was a heavy box, well the very next day, I was out in the garden mooching and I looked up and Jesus H. Christ, I saw the most hideous looking thing attached to his garden shed. It was a plastic pissing owl. It didn't even look real, for starters its eyes were like massive, over exaggerated things, and it got worse: when it got dark, they shone and looked like freak zombie eyes. If I hadn't known it was the owl, it would have scared the shit of me.

Who orders a plastic munter owl online and then puts it up on their shed, FFS? Well if this continues, I am just going to piss on his parcels - he will soon get the message then, when his items stink of my piss! HA, yeah that's a good plan.

Anyway, I need to go and find Mum, I need to relieve myself and then I need a snack. My blood sugars are low, I am sure of it…

She was still in the kitchen after answering the door, so my luck was in. I gave her the nod with my head towards the back door and whined, she knew straight away, god I am good. My telepathy is quite incredible really, so off I went outside, but goddam it was cold! I am sure it's time for snow soon, but if it gets too cold, the white wondrous stuff won't fall, so it needs to warm up a little… This frost under my paws is murder, my feet sometimes slip, and god if I fall over and break my leg or hip, well that's Christmas over for starters, so need to be careful when cocking the old Arthur's ritus leg.

Ooooo that's better, now time for my afternoon snack, what does Mum have in store for me today? Oh ok, not bad, not bad, it's one of my grass sticks, nom nom nomm. I am off munching on this, little happy tail wag as I go.

I have just been on Twitter again, and I am now following a pig, and she is gorgeous, people. I know, odd, right, that I should like a pig, but I think it's because we share so many similarities. She has an enormous appendage like mine, and LOVES food, and of course sleeps a lot, so what's not to like? I even sent a video clip of myself rolling on my back with my udders out, making grunting piggy sounds. Oh she loved it, and in fact it has been retweeted. I am going to be a superstar, I can feel it.

However, for now, snooze time. Dad is home and Mum is cooking (better be something good), so nothing is happening, see ya later.

I have been woken up by some strange smell. It's not chicken, or my fave, beef, but smells fishy. I don't like it, uurrgghh! It is like a vile explosion of wet kippers. WTF? I hope Ginger Bastard hasn't been invited round - why else would Mum cook fish? Disgusting. I definitely do not want any of that, I will stay here in my comfy bed. My nostrils will have this stench in them now for weeks, thank you very much!

Well, the only way I could escape the smell was naturally to sleep through, and so it is Thursday, and what is odd is Dad is here. If he has lost his job, Mum will go insane. This happened once, many years ago, he got made redundant and was moaning for weeks that he was on some scrap heap… Even I couldn't console him and I tried people, I really did. I would climb up on his lap and lick his face, I would lie with him when he was on his computer thingy (not as good as my dogpad!) and help him search for jobs, but he was a lost cause. He grew more facial hair than I have ever seen (it put my beard to shame), and he took to wearing these elasticated trouser things, which Granddad wore one year on Christmas Day, but that's another story.

Finally Mum had had enough, and said if he didn't pull himself together, he could live in the fecking garage out of her sight, and take me with him. Well I wasn't having that people, I mean firstly what had I done? I had a job, I was chief barker, magpie-chaser, birdwatcher and head of farting, so I don't know what Mum's problem was with me. Dad yeah I could understand, he looked sadder than Bassett, and that's saying something.

So, he had to shave, which I sat and watched - it was fascinating to see him emerge out of this fur. Then he got dressed and went to see a man about a job! That day was a good day people, my Dad he came back all proud and with a puffed- out chest, and Mum was smiling again, thank god (she's very ugly when not), and harmony was restored. Dad had found himself a new job, and it turned out it was better than the one he lost. So the moral of the story is, don't be a pussy bastard, and just get on with it, Capiche?

Anyway, back to today, and why is Dad here? I need to investigate, so I am off to find out…

It's ok people, he has not lost his job, thank Christ. No, he is doing some last-minute Christmas shopping before the big day, which is next week, YIPPEEEEE… Anyway I wonder what last-minute gifts he is buying, there better be some for me.

Oh Mum is yelling for me, why she can't just shout normal? I don't know, I'm not deaf, yet, unlike Granddad Potato, who frequently misses most conversations these days. Christmas Day will be fun, ha! So I am off for my walk, back soon.

I've just got back from my walk and I am splitting my sides. There is another newbie, or least I haven't seen this chap before… I would know if I had, because he walks very camp and his fur is all puffed up, but get this, when I found out what he was I literally laughed in his face - he said he was a shih tzu! I said, "a what, a shit zoo?" and I was like "isn't that just a zoo with no animals? ha ha ha" - he said I was a dumb asshole and trotted off. I think I heard his owner say "come on Fitz, time to go", what kind of camp name is that!! I don't think me and Fitz will be making friends anytime soon - no sense of humour.

Just checked Twitter… Stuffington was feeling down today, as it's getting closer to Christmas, so I cheered her up with my story of Fitz, and she found it very funny. I was like, I know, I am very amusing. I also now have a couple more followers, one is a pet magazine - ooo interesting, maybe they are looking for their next front page spread, I would certainly fill it with my udders, ha ha. That would fly off the shelves! Maybe I need to tweet them my best side, yes I'm going to do it, but before I do I need food. I can hear my belly grumbling… back in a mo…

I am suitably satisfied for now… but I am sure Mum put less in my bowl, I need to watch that. If she thinks I am dieting again she can piss off, not this close to Christmas anyway, in fact NEVER. I shall live my life with udders and I shall be proud of them, so how about a treat? I haven't had one of my dental sticks for days and days, standards are slipping in this place. Jeez, don't let me have to run away, Mum would be heartbroken. In fact as I am her Number One she would curl up and die, that's for sure, so gimme a stick.

I win, nom nom nommmmmmm! See ya later people, I am in stick paradise, will report back later if I can be bothered.

Oh treats today: 3, and this stick, HA!

Birds: like I said ZERO

Chapter 9 - IT'S CHRISSSTTTMMMASSS!!

Diary

I just couldn't be bothered with diary or Twitter these last few days, and in fact you are not going to believe this people but… wait for it… wait…

ITTT'SSSSS CHRISTMAS!!! Wake up, wake up, wake up! I need to stick my tongue up Mum's nose to get her attention, I am scrambling over the pillow to get to her, ooommmpff! I have plonked myself full weight on her chest, ha ha she can't move, in I go… Oh don't be like that Mum, Santa's been! so get up! I want my breakfast first, then a walk, then my presents.

Oh no, no, no, no you are not shooing me, how very dare you! I am not sitting downstairs on my own today, so I will wait here at the end of the bed - you do what you have to do, I will lie very still. OMG world record Dad, that was like 2 minutes, must be because it's Christmas. Mum is lucky.

Oooo Mum is getting up, off we go. "Oh I wish it could be Christmas every day!" I cannot wait for my present, and to see what shit Mum has bought Dad this year, always gets me laughing, but first breakfast please. I need to set myself up for the day's festivities and the arrival of Nanny Hammy and Granddad potato, to see what they are wearing this year, as last year Granddad had on these absurd ugly elasticated things. I nearly choked on my tongue, they were god awful. His explanation, I heard him say to Mum, was that he felt comfortable in them and there was room for his dinner. I thought, jeez how much food are you going to eat? There was enough elastic in them to make a bungee for an elephant, again why do you oldies resort to ugly dressing? Stop please, it's unpleasant on the eye.

Anyway, back to my breakfast, it better be the good stuff… Oh, oh, I can smell sausage pieces, Mum has pulled out all the stops! I am off people, see you soon. Oh, Merry Christmas, in case I forget later.

That's breakfast done, now for the Christmas morning walk. Mum has stuffed the turkey and he/she is in the oven. A little bit of saliva has dribbled out of my mouth people, at the thought of moist turkey later, nom nom nom, so off we go, back in a mo.

Dad even came with us this morning, he must be feeling energetic! And what a walk, we passed so many of the freaks this morning, I lost count, and Dad well he didn't know half of them, so they were all just saying "Merry Christmas" to Mum. Then we saw the Pugly Club, ha ha ha ha ha, Dad had to hide his face, get this, are you ready… They were BOTH wearing antlers! I shit you not, his Dad had on these giant things, bouncing round on his fat head, and mushed-up bastard had miniature ones on. I started with my wheezing I was laughing so hard, Mum had to bend down to check on me, but people it gets worse, oh yes.

We passed Frankfurter (he was quite sedate, dressed in a plain red jacket), but it was Douglas, OMG, he went into overdrive bark, I have never seen him like it! But what is worse is he had on a ridiculous Santa hat, I mean seriously, were they all trying to kill me off this morning?

I shouted, "WTF Doogal, is your Dad a joker?" Bark bark bark bark, yeah, yeah dumbo, you look like an idiot. We passed Ian Beagle and Bassett, he still looked sad, poor guy, and then the best bit of the walk by far, SHIT ZOO chap, who was dressed as… wait…

An ELF, and did he look absurd! He had the hat with pointy ears, the little midget elf coat on his back, and he even had some ridiculous elf shoes on his paws… I was like WTF, what kind of bad karma shit did you do in a previous life for your Dad to do this to you? HA HA HA, that was it, I was done, I had to stand still and catch my breath. When I could finally speak again I shouted, "I bet you have low ELF-esteem, don't you?" Oh, he was not amused.

Sadly, we didn't see Ginger Bastard, hope that dirty pussy ain't buried himself in his own shit!

I couldn't wait to tweet my morning's exploits, and wish all my furry ones a Happy Happy Christmas. Twitter was in overdrive this morning. All the furry ones are excited, and many have already had some presents. Fat cat had a new scratching pole, it was a super-sized one, fecking enormous it was, but I kept those comments to myself. The piggy I follow, who is my fave, had tweeted a pic of herself dressed as a reindeer, captioned "Pigs Can Fly" - oooo I like that, so retweeted it.

I then tweeted Stuffington and wished her a Merry Christmas, and said I hoped she wasn't too down, but in fact she tweeted right back, and said she was happy as she had a new view - she was now seated by the back door and could see into the garden.

I then tweeted my piece de resistance! Me dressed as Father Christmas, with the caption "It's Santa PAWS!" Oh come on people, I'm killing it - I amuse you, admit it. That bad boy got retweeted over 20 times, and got so many likes, wow. Anyway it's time for presents, so I shall report back people, what shit Dad has got. ha ha ha ha

People, you are not going to believe it, well let me start by saying, my presents - yes the plural, PRESENTS - were A.M.A.Z.I.N.G.! I had a new sparkly red collar, and before you say anything it is not camp, as it has studs on it, so piss off! I also had a turkey chew thing, nom nom nom, that was devoured in like 30 seconds, but then big drum roll, I got a new toy, and it is the best toy yet! It is round like bally, but it's disguised as a snowman, and wait for it… it flashes when it rolls! OMG the hours of fun I am going to have with that today… whoooooooo hooooo! Mum is THE BEST, as I know it wasn't tight arse Dad who bought me these.

Talking of Dad, his presents had me rolling! Mum excelled herself this year people, first present he opened was a new lunch bag!!! What is he, like seven or something? ha ha. It got worse, he also got some socks, and a god awful hat with what looked like dog ears on the sides. HE IS NOT walking me with that on, I do not want to be the talk of ridicule, I do the piss taking round here.

But I have to tell you this people, and this is so funny, you will need to hang onto your sides… After Dad had opened his shit, I mean presents, he gave his to Mum, and I thought, oooo this will be good, he buys great gifts, well, so I thought. Mum had asked Dad for a new iPad (like my dogpad, but bigger), as she said hers was damaged (I think she was lying and just wanted the newer model!). Anyway, Dad gave Mum this box and she was all like, "Oh you haven't!" and " Oh you didn't!" - ooooo exciting, even I want to know now what is in the box, so I was jumping up Mum's leg… Anyway when she finally opened it, you could have cut the tension with a knife!!

Inside was NOT an iPad, people, but an ACTUAL EYE PAD, like what you put on someone's eye when it has been injured. I was laughing so hard, I thought my udders would explode - I did not know my Dad could be so funny. Mum's face was like WTF, but then she did burst out laughing, people. Phew, that was a close call; I thought dinner would be ruined!!

And to be fair to Dad, he did then produce the actual real iPad, so Mum was happy, and all in all, present giving this year was hilarious. I wonder what time Nanny Hammy and Granddad potato will be here - I might have a little nap while I am waiting, see ya later……

I have awoken to the smell of roast turkey people, I am a big sack of dribbling drooling saliva, ooo! And also, I can hear Nanny and Granddad, they better not have started without me, selfish bastards. I'm gonna get me some of that turkey action - "when life reaches out with a moment like this, it's a sin if you don't reach back" (De Niro). I am sure that is what he meant, go get the turkey, son.

Turkey, turkey, here turkey, turkey, come to poppa, YES, thanks be to baby Jesus, there is turkey in my bowl… It's time for the dance people, I'm tapping, I'm wagging, I'm squeaking… "You will have to wait Rupert, Nanny has gone to the loo" - OMG like WTF has this got to do with me? and uuuurrrggh, too much information! I don't wish to have that image, just gimme me my turkey bitch, sorry, I mean Mum… NO, I have got to wait until everyone is seated, well may as well go tweet a quick pic in that case…

Ok thank you, everyone is seated, Granddad looks half cut, and Nanny is swaying a bit also… Jeez, people, it's only 4 p.m., WTF? I can see how this night is going to go, but for now it's turkey heaven, nom nommmm nommmmmmmm nommmmmm nommmmmmmm, I cannot even begin (nomm) to tell you (nommmmm), the divine moistness of heaven (nommm) - this is… can't talk…

I'm back, but let me say this people, Granddad potato has shamed himself. The fart he did at the table nearly made Dad sick, and well Nanny Hammy choked on her sprout (yuk green hideous bastards)… It was the vilest, most putrid-smelling fart I ever did smell, and that is rich coming from me. I had to go and get in comfy bed. Granddad is now in the lounge, prostrate with big zzzzzzzz's coming out his mouth, and his elasticated monstrosities are pulled up nearly to his chin. Good god, it's a sight for sore eyes, I might have to tweet it… Yes I'm going to, ha ha ha ha, I have added the caption "Stuffed Potato, anyone?" No real activity on Twitter, maybe everyone is snoozing… Well I am going to play with Snowman, my new toy. That should entertain me for a few minutes ha.

Oh dear, people, Snowman is in the bin!! Let's just say oops, and who makes these crap toys ?, It lasted all of 6 minutes and 25 seconds. I nudged it around a bit and became fascinated with the flashing lights, but then they were like seriously pissing me off, so I thought, I need to get inside it to get them out… I then bit into Snowman with my teeth, and I did not stop until the outer layer was ripped off, and the insides were ripped out. That soon stopped that bastard HA, in your face flashing snowman, IDIOT!

Mum was of course not happy. Dad was laughing, and even shouted "Go on Rupert", which did egg me on I must admit. So Snowman is no more, he has gone to rest with Froggy No Eyes, RIP both, thank you for the good times.

I need a snooze - all these festivities have left me so very sleepy, I shall report back later people, off you go too, have a little nap…

Jesus, Mary and Joseph, I have slept for 4 hours straight, and missed the entertainment. Even Nanny Hammy and Granddad potato have gone home, obviously all the turkey has gone!! I bet Nanny has some in her handbag! Anyway I was in such a deep sleep, I even had a dream, and Mum had to nudge me to see if I was ok, as apparently I was kicking my legs and whimpering. That must have been the part when I was running and chasing squirrelly bastard, but for some strange reason I had Froggy No Eyes strapped to my back, how weird! Anyway now that I am awake, I shall just gently ease myself off the sofa, and go and check Twitter. Whoooooeee, I have kind of belly-flopped onto the rug, ooo this feels nice on my udders, I shall just stretch out a bit and pull myself along… MAAAYYYbe I could make it all the way to the other side… ha ha, I've done it.

Right Twitterati, what gives? Oh, Stuffington has been tweeting random shots, even one of her with tinsel round her neck… Hope she is ok, looks a little worse for wear! OMG, moving on, I have another new follower and it is another pet magazine, and get this, they are from the U. S. of A., that is it baby, I am going global! I can see it now, #tubbyfootstool takes America by storm, he and his furry warriors capture the hearts of millions! Oh yes, I am going to send them my best pic yet.

Well I tweeted a shot of me in a shirt and tie, and added the caption "It's been a Ruff day"… let's see what response that gets. While I am waiting I will just double-check the turkey situation, back soon…

Greedy, goddam bastards, all the turkey has gone, not a scrap left! I told you, didn't I people, that Nanny Hammy has some in her handbag, and she will be eating that for her supper, while little old me has to starve, filthy rotten selfish twats, there I've said it! I am in a serious sulk, and also have checked Twitter and that magazine hasn't even liked my pic, well they can piss off too. I am going to lie back down, or better still maybe it's time for night night time.

GO AWAY, it is too early, and Christmas is over, well it is in this house anyway. No turkey, no more presents, no more fun, so what is the point? And I don't get why it's called Boxing Day either, dumb name, I mean do people go around punching each other? Ha ha yes probably, too much time spent with relatives you hate! So I am not moving, now shove over Dad, make room for little old me.

PPPPfffffttt, excuse me, that must have been the turkey, and the fact that I stole a bit of stuffing off Granddad potato's plate, pppfffttt, pppffftt, oooo better out than in. "Jesus H. Christ, is that you?" Mum is shouting at Dad, ha ha ha, she thinks it's him and is now getting up, muttering "dirty sod!"

Awww bliss, just me and Dad for a change… I shall press myself close to his back and stretch out, now Mum is out, yeah this is the life… Hang on though, hang on… I am sure I can smell turkey, this better not be a joke. No, my bionic nostrils can definitely smell turkey, I need to get downstairs quick and see if this is real.

OOOOmmmmpppf, I am off the bed, a quick rub around the rug, grunting sounds feel appropriate here, oh yeah, just a bit more scooting and then I can go downstairs.

People, harmony has been restored and Boxing Day is not ruined. Mum (my saviour) had saved me some bastard turkey for my breakfast, and it is now sitting in my bowl waiting for me, silently taunting me with its divine smell. OMG OMG OMG I am so happy! I even checked Twitter and that American magazine finally liked my pic, and so this day is turning out to be the best yet, but I need a walk, so have to go… Gorra get back quick for turkey lurkey, nom nomm nommmmmm…

The walk was borrrriing, however I did pass Ginger Bastard, and get this, he had a companion with him, some shabby tabby looking thing (looked a bit mangy to me). I shouted, "Alright Ginger Bastard! have a good Christmas? who's your new fwend?" He looked at me in utter disgust and said, "Meet Clarence, he is staying with us over Christmas", and then he said, "I hate him, and his Mum, and god awful snotty screaming munter kids".

Oh dear, I thought, sounds like Boxing Day is going to live up to its name in Ginger Bastard's house… to be fair I would hate that, to be descended upon by riff raff relatives. Oh god, it gives me the shivers. Glad Mum and Dad are antisocial bastards.

Back home and now time for my turkey, gimme gimme gimme, ooooooo nom nommmmmmmm… I shall speak later people…

That was scrummy, Mum is the best, and now Dad is up, grunting and looking for food. He's like a potato caveman, and what's with the scratching of his nut sack? uurrrggh, does he need a scratching pole? Stop it! At least I rub myself along the rug with dignity, and besides YOU BASTARDS STOLE MY NUTS!!! Now I am like left with these udders - I feel like saying I have nipples, now milk me! I need to check Twitter, see what all the egomaniacs are up to…

Well Twitter was full of tweets about people's Christmas Day exploits, and who got what and who went where. I tweeted Stuffington and asked if she was ok… she replied with a tweet of her and a new stuffed friend, I was like who is THAT?! It was a stuffed chicken, and his name Mr Chicken, of course! She said he was to keep her company. Oh right, thanks, well I hope you and Mr Chicken bastard will be very happy.

Tweeted a joke, "What is black and white and goes, ha ha plonk, ha ha plonk?… A penguin laughing his head off!"

Oh come on, this shit is funny, NO? Ok then what about this…

"What do you call a dinosaur with no eyes?

Doyouthinkhesawus!" Ha ha ha ha. Oh piss off.

I am in need of a snooze, all this tweeting and turkey has made me sleepy, and before you ask, NO I am not dieting for the New Year. CAPICHE?

I have been rudely awoken from my slumber by music, I think Dad is playing one of his CDs, some group from the 80's (he only likes 80's music). It's ok, I think I can make out the words, "more than this", or something like that, but it's a bit howly for me. I prefer it when Mum plays Glen Campbell or Johnny Cash, I am a cowdog at heart, especially with these udders… Well as I am awake I may as well go and have me a mosey on through to the kitchen, maybe sniff out a biscuit.

I got me a biscuit, people, but it was a bit stale. I think Mum needs to sort out my treat drawer, I cannot be eating cardboard tasting shit, that is abuse. Well this Boxing Day is now becoming a bit boring, I don't have a new toy (RIP Snowman), Twitter is dead, and Nanny Hammy and
Grandad potato won't be here until later. Oh yeah I forgot to say, they are coming for snacks later!

I bet they are only coming because as per usual, their cupboards are bare. They will eat us out of house and home, the scavengers.

So nothing more to say or do, other than have a little… nap!

Holy crap, Nanny Hammy and Grandad potato are here already, and jeez, Nanny is dancing with Dad, STOP IT, STOP IT NOW! They look like two swaying weebles with legs, OMG has Dad been drinking? He's now singing, and Nanny is joining

in, this is serious abuse to my ears - CALL THE SHOW, EMERGENCY, dog's ears are bleeding all over rug…
OH Christ on a bike, Mum is now singing with Nanny, and Granddad looks suitably unimpressed, maybe his ears are bleeding too… It is the worst sound ever, something about "cars as big as bars, and rivers of gold" (uurrgghh, why? has someone pissed in them?). Oh god, Dad is pulling a strange face at Mum now and singing to her, "you were handsome, you were pretty", well that's not nice saying she WAS pretty, I think she still is. I am going to bark, that might stop them.

IT DID NOT STOP THEM…. Mum picked me up and started twirling me around… Oh please, I begged, put me down! She didn't, so I farted on her hand, PPPPFFFFTTTTTT, it was a corker, her face was a picture, HA HA HA serves you right.

Now them lot are all playing the card game, GIN, so I have tucked myself away in comfy bed. I have no desire to listen to the drunken ramblings, even Mum is gin-fuelled now and talking shite! I can see what kind of night I am in for. I hope Nanny Hammy and Grandad potato are not sleeping here, it's a tight squeeze as it is in the big bed - with all five of us, well that's pushing it!

Well, Nanny Hammy and Granddad potato have left, in a taxi, as Granddad was very drunk, even though he drove here, so he will be in trouble no doubt. He could hardly stand, it was hilarious. Mum had to help get him in the taxi and he bashed his head on the door, ha ha ha, smashed potato!

SSHHHHHHHH, we are in bed, the big night night one, and Mum is making her dragon sounds, and Dad is doing his impression of a train, me I am lying between them… OMG SHUT THE F UP! Can't a dog get any sleep round here? Jeez. I am going to prod Mum in the back with my paws, yes it's worked, just Dad now… if I can just turn round, ooo turning, this is fun, ooo might have to try and dig me a hole in the mattress! Yes, I shall do that, oooommpff, ahhh, much better, and as a result Dad has shut up… Quiet now people, sleepy time. Goodnight.

Get up, get up, get up, I need a wee, oh no you don't, get your stinking rancid buffalo breath away from me, I am not kissing either of you today! I just want a wee, a walk, breakfast, and a snooze, in that order, now.

Thank god, Mum has finally managed to stumble downstairs and let me out. I am suitably relieved. That was because they didn't let me out last night, too pissing drunk, selfish BASTARDS.

Right, who is taking me for my morning walk, come on, come on… Oh, Dad is. This could be interesting! Off we go, see you in a mo.

That was hilarious people, firstly Dad hadn't properly woken up and was out walking in his pyjamas, the shame! and secondly the Pugly club stopped to talk to him. I was like WTF, they never talk to Mum, but he was asking Dad if we had a good Christmas. I was like, piss off and don't be so nosy! Mushed-up bastard tried to come and sniff my arse, but I soon told him, I said, mate get any closer to my rear end with that pugly face of yours and I will shit in your eyes! He soon backed off, but what I hadn't noticed before was how fecking big his eyes are, MAN they are like giant glass marbles, all popped out and shit, makes him look like he is constantly straining for a poo, ha ha ha. Maybe that can be his new nickname, "Poo Strain", ha.

We passed Ginger Bastard, his companion Clarence had obviously gone back to whatever stone he came out from. I could tell Ginger Bastard was pleased, he was back to trying to swipe and hiss at me. Dad was like, "ha, Rupert, who's your new friend?" I barked loudly, HE IS NO FRIEND OF MINE! Ginger Bastard thought this was really funny, until I shouted "shed!" at him, that soon shut him up, HA in your face.

Other than that, it was fairly uneventful, and we were soon back. Mum had my breakfast ready, I should think so too, and it was nice and warm and cosy inside. Oooo nap time, methinks later.

I did check my Twitter, and tweeted a few pics of me, myself and I, who else! I put one on of me mid-yawn, and added the caption "just told myself a joke". Stuffington liked that… oh yeah, Stuffington and Mr Chicken are no more - she discovered he liked cocks more! - so she had him evacuated, he now resides in the closet under stairs. That's harsh, I tweeted, but she replied and said he deserved it! I decided to follow a wildlife protection group, can't have too many people to contact in case of an emergency or neglect, take note Mum!

All the events of the last few days have left me exhausted so I need to get up on the sofa and snuggle, uninterrupted if you please, so see ya later.

NO NO NO NO just NO, why can't a dog just get a snooze? The bastard vacuum is out, and of course it is the monster snake, and I need to bark at him. So naturally I have to get off the sofa, ooomppf, rub my non-existent dognots along the rug first, then scoot myself around and around… Now I am ready to face the black snake.

Ha ha I bit him, one-nil to me, you bastard! Oh Mum is coming at me again, whoa, not round my rear! Stop it, oh god please end this now, I am exhausted from barking… Oh thank you, finally he is going back to his den, now let me just check Twitter… OH interesting, a new follower, and it is another dawgie. Oh and it is a she dawgie, and people she is chubby like me - whoooooo hooooo, this is great news! We can share fat stories.

I have tweeted her… Oh you want to know what she is, well I think minger or something, no wait, wait mongrel! yes that's it, and her name is Clarice, I am not making this shit up. I naturally then told her of my serial killer patch, ooo she loved that, wanted to know what was in there, I said it was a bit cold to check but I would keep her informed.

Oh Stuffington tweeted and said Mr Chicken was back out of the closet! She said he was actually quite entertaining, and gave good fashion advice. I said maybe he could help me cover my udders up. ERM, honey, he said, no amount of material could hide those babies. Cheeky bastard, he wants to watch I don't roast him! Pecking fecker. Anyway I am hungry, so I am just going to sneak, ninja style, into the kitchen and see if I can get me some treat action.

Got me a chewy stick, nom nommmm, Mum couldn't resist my big brown eyes. Going to snuggle for a bit now with Dad, as he has to go back to work tomorrow, and again N.O. spells no, piss off, I have no desire to embark on some fitness regime or any such nonsense, so you judge all you like, I'm not bothered! Now I am sleeping… sssssshhhhhh.

Stats for the whole of Christmas

Treats: like a hundred baby, Ok maybe not that many, but lots

Still no birds, or pigeon bastards. (I wonder where they go over winter, probably some rat den!)

Monday

Dad has gone to work very reluctantly, I think he was sad to leave me, to be honest. Mum didn't seem too fussed though - as soon as he got out of the bed, she star fished and stretched out. I joined in, and it was soooo much fun, then I went in for a nostril lick. "Eurgh, gerroff boy", no, no, no, no, come here! Ha ha Mum is getting up now, so I can do me a bit of scooting. I shall await the call for my walk, oh I wonder if Nanny Hammy will be here today.

Yeah, Nanny Hammy is here, come to eat all our food have ya? She did give me a lish lush treat to eat, so, eat away Nanny, eat away. I have been on my walk, and it wasn't very entertaining… Checked Twitter, Stuffington had tweeted a pic of herself, dressed in some god awful silk robe thing, said it was her and Mr Chicken's lounge wear - dear god, what is he turning her into, some Fag Hag? I tweeted and said she wasn't in an episode of Sex and the City, and Mr Chicken was NOT MR Big! Ha Ha that has had quite a few likes already. I need to snooze on the sofa… Nanny Hammy is still here, gorging, but I shall see if I can sneak on.

Well, that didn't go as planned. I tried jumping up, but only made it half way, and I could feel my udders slipping… Mum tried to grab me, bitch nearly broke my arm, careful I have Arthur's ritus! Jeez, then Nanny rear-ended me (good god, the shame!). They did eventually manage to plonk me between them, but it felt odd, so I had to circle several times until karma was restored, and then snooze.

I can vaguely hear Nanny Hammy telling Mum how difficult it was to get Granddad potato to bed Boxing night, she said he pissed himself, the dirty rotten bastard, and she had to change his underpants, and the last time she saw something that small was when she was young and used to go fishing with her granddad. I have no idea what she was on about, but it made my Mum laugh anyway. Oh I forgot to say they picked the car up the next morning, but didn't stay, something about being hunger-over… Yeah, I thought, that's because you ate all our food, greedy bastards.

Well I am drifting here, so could be a while people… I shall report back later.

Nanny Hammy has gone, and Dad is back and I am still prostrate on the sofa, some snooze that was! It won't be long before it's the New Year, but in all honesty I really don't know what is new about it. Might get up and check Twitter, ooo head is heavy, aww bollocks to it, I am going back to sleep, wake me if anything exciting happens, or if there is food.

Chapter 10 - What's New About It?

Diary

Good morning, or IS IT really? Christmas is officially over people, and it's the New Year, but what the hell is new about it? It's just the same for me: get up, walk (well, waddle), hunt for food (yeah alright stop laughing, I am sure my ancestors had to hunt), BEG for treats, sleep, and check my Twitter. So, what's new about that?

What I do know is that last night was a traumatic event, and I wish all you bastards who go out and buy fireworks would seriously piss off and go and live on the moon (or your-anus!) or somewhere far, far away from me. It's totally unnecessary - here's an idea, send the money you waste on those explosives to an animal charity or good cause, and then just turn to the human next to you and say Happy New Year, instead of standing outside at some ungodly hour, watching them blow up.

Rant over, I need to wake Mum so she can see to my needs, why isn't she up? She usually gets up at a ridiculous hour, FFS. Right, time for the Rupert special, methinks! I'm tapping her head with my paw, ooo she's waking up, it's working… I shall apply pressure and scratch a bit. Oh she didn't like that, she's shouting, "stop it Rupert, paw your Dad!" NO I don't want to, he has dragon breath, it smells like a camel has shit in his mouth overnight, so no thank you. Give me your attention, I will continue to paw you and now I shall lick your ears and face, GET UP...

Ha ha ha who's the ruler, the king (of comedy), the Numero Uno? Me Me Me! Mum finally relented and is up, and I am wearing my new sparkly collar today for my walk, I am so gonna rub it in everyone's faces… oh come on, let's go…

That was a great walk! I actually trotted a bit today in my new collar! Passed Ginger Bastard, who was sitting licking himself, uurrrghhh, he is one dirty bastard. Passed shit zoo guy, Fitz, he was also sporting a new collar, but get this, it was pink, ha ha ha, what a girl colour. Also saw Douglas, the New Year hasn't changed his dumb habits, same old same old. I think I might have to encourage Mum to take me on a new route, or come out later. Anyway that was it this morning.

Back home now and ready for my breakfast, but first I am going to check Twitter, see what my furry friends made of last night, and wish Stuffington my BF a Happy New Year, see if the Fag
Hag is still dressed in silk! Also will tweet Clarice, the fat bitch - we have become good

friends, and when I can get out to my patch, will tweet her my items.

Well, breakfast this morning resembled tiny pebbles of shit, and at first I thought, OH NO you don't, you wouldn't dare put me back on the diet crappy stuff without consultation, but no, it didn't seem like diet food.

Two reasons: 1) it tasted of lamb (I like me a bit of sheep!) and vegetables and 2) it wasn't dry. Also because it was small and compact, I could stuff more in my gob, and at one point I resembled Nanny Hammy, ha ha ha ha, so pebble shit can stay. Nice one Mum.

I am in need of a little snooze, and as it's New Year Day, Dad is here, so will snuggle next to him on the sofa, see what crap he's watching. Be back soon, don't miss me too much.

As I knew you would be missing me, I am back, but briefly. I have to whisper, ssshhhhhhh, I can hear Mum shouting for me, so quickly. Dad was watching a crappy old film called the Elmo or something, I thought it was about a muppet, turns out not so, but I got bored, anyway… ssssssshhhhhhIIITTTTTT.

Mum is still calling me… I am feigning ignorance and pretending I am deaf, as I know what she wants. "Rupert, RUPERT, RUPPPERRTT!" Oh bollocks, now she is coming to find me.

Ha ha, I have gone under the dining table and she can't reach me… No no no, I am NOT having my nails clipped, they are just fine. Oh wait she has a treat now, ooo it's my favourite, a denta stick, bastard, now I have to come out, nom nommm nommmm.

WHOA, hang on there, Mum, let me at least digest my stick before you assault me! Off we go upstairs, brushy time and nail clipper time - ABUSE, call for help.

Well brushy time was soothing, I sat all relaxed whilst Mum brushed me with Basil, but I only let her do my front paws, HA! I wriggled too much for the back ones, and besides, it's not as if I have talons, I am not a budgie, so piss off. I have now escaped and have gone for a scoot around the landing. I like to do this sometimes as the carpet is nice and soft and doesn't cause friction burns, and let me tell you people, they hurt.

I will check my Twitter, and then embark on a trip outside to see what I can mooch at, but I think the ground is still a bit hard for burying. I cannot wait for spring.

Checked Twitter, it seems lots of people (or idiots, I shall call them) are starting on New Year's resolutions. Fools, the lot of them, especially those who are on diets; won't catch me starting that malarkey again. OH dear God, someone has tweeted a pic of himself dressed in a tight vest holding a puppy, yeah mate the puppy is great, but you look like a giant dick and nobody needs to see you and/or your bulging biceps. Oh talking of vests, that has reminded me of the time Dad lost a bit of weight and bought a multi pack, ha ha ha.

He thought he was Rambo, and said he would wear it all summer. Mum was like "no way are you coming out in that, with me". Personally I thought he looked like a chubby Bruce Willis, but what do I know? Anyway he lost, and the multi pack mysteriously disappeared, like many more of his items of clothing! Ha ha.

Well all that exertion of trying to escape Mum and then wriggling has left me feeling somewhat sleepy, so no choice but to go back to the sofa with Dad… I hope to god the film has finished. OMG, it's still on and I can hear Mum saying, "for Christ sake, you watch this every year, turn it off!" Yeah Dad turn it off, or at least see if there is any Game of Thrones on, or David Attenborough, or my fave, Goodfellas, and I can at least act out some of the parts like I do.

Oh ok, put some music on, yeah this is more like it, Glen Campbell, "Witchy Line Man". I like this one, ha ha, Mum is singing into Basil again, at Dad this time. He is looking suitably annoyed, oh he's shouting, "you've turned off a classic for this crap?" Yeah Dad we have! I'm gonna bark at his feet, get him up dancing… ha ha it's worked, he is up, OH he's gone to the kitchen… ooo hang on though, it could mean an opportunity for another sneaky treat, wish me luck…

Good result, people, Dad didn't know Mum had already enticed me with a dental stick, he was too busy lounging on the sofa, and so he has just given me another one, and it's the grass stick one, nom nommmm nomm nommm, oh this is heaven! Oops, he's getting told off now by Mum. WHOA, what did she just say? Back up there, broad, BACK UP…

NO, PISS OFF, GET STUFFED, SOMEONE CALL FOR HELP, ABUSE! What a crafty sneaky cow, she has decided on her own - well no, with Dad, the traitor - that they are putting me on a diet, and that food I ate this morning was in fact diet shit. I knew something was odd, my spidery senses alerted me.

How dare they do this to me without any consultation, well I might just go on a hunger strike! Yeah, yeah, alright, I can hear laughter… Well I have been well and truly duped, and feel very hurt, and now I can also hear Nanny Hammy and Granddad potato. No food here, you scavengers, only pebble shit, you're welcome to that. I am going to my comfy bed, DO NOT DISTURB, unless it's a treat.

Nanny Hammy tried to console me, and said it was for my own good… Well what about your own good, eh greedy guts, coming here stuffing biscuits in your trap? I turned my head away in disgust, talk to the paw. Oh dear God, can't I just sulk in peace? Now Granddad potato is bending down, ppppffftttt, ha, ha, he's farted. "Arthur, for god's sake!" Yes Arthur, go and fart in your own house and leave me be.

Well, they didn't stay long, probably found out about pebble shit, and turned their noses up. Mum is calling me now, FFS WHAT? Oh we are going for a walk, like now. Erm WHY? Exercise, apparently. Well I ain't running, that's for sure.

Just got back, and jeez, Mum made me RUN, my udders grazed the floor and my Arthur's ritus was killing me, so I have collapsed on the floor (pretend collapse, don't panic), just so I don't have to continue with that torture. HA HA Mum is panicking, she thinks she has broken me. YEAH IN your face, look what you have done, now ugly cry.

Dad has come to check on me, "come here my boy, what has your Mum done to you?" Ha ha ha ha, I am wheezing now, from laughing so much. Oh no Mum is properly ugly crying now, really does think I am broken, hang on wait, I heard V.E.T.! OH NO, I am up twirling round and barking now, see I am fine, it's all good, stop crying now, that's it, come and give me a love.

Maybe that will teach her, and we can stop this diet shit and exercise regime. Oh I need a snooze, but first I'll just check Twitter.

Ha ha I have tweeted a poll, and I put my options as:

Stay fat but cute

Diet and DIE OF NEGLECT

So far "Stay fat but cute" is winning in the poll - see, everyone loves a chubby guy. Tweeted Clarice and she said she voted "stay fat", not surprisingly, being a little on the rotund side herself. She told me I should hide my food for midnight snacks. Great idea, thanks BF.

I am definitely going for a snooze now, so only wake for me for a) treats, b) food and c) treats, CAPICHE?

Ha ha I have slept through, and also I have conceded, people, and reluctantly I am sticking to the diet and eating the pebble crap, and I am walking slightly further. In fact this morning on my walk, I noticed my udders weren't swinging with so much gusto, and when we passed the Pugly club I heard his owner say to Mum, "diet's working". I don't know if he was referring to mine or Mum's (as she is also on a regime), and I thought, nosey bastard, piss off, but my inner self was rather chuffed.

Spotted Frankfurter, he was sporting some kind of scarf round his neck, made him look like a tied up salami, ha ha. Then I passed Shitzoo and had to hold my wee in, as he was sporting a cashmere jumper. WTF, mate, you already have a jumper, it's called your FUR, you thick twat. Seriously, some folks. Anyway that was it this morning, back home now checking Twitter.

Clarice is concerned I am wasting away, I've tweeted her a pic of my rear, she tweeted back reassured and said she likes big butts and she cannot lie, ha ha. Stuffington my BF and Mr Chicken have had an argument, on Twitter of all places - she called him a pecking queen, he retaliated and said at least he was a sassy queen, and wasn't just a stuffed sack cloth full of wool! I came to Stuffy's rescue and said that at least she had a label, not like charity shop chicken HA HA.

Ooo he didn't like that, but I don't care can't him abusing my BF.

Well I need a snooze… It is Saturday after all, and Dad is here still! He hasn't even bothered with badminton - looks like that's another attempt down the shitter, unless he embarks on another new regime! like Mum, who is also now on a diet (she needs to speak to Nanny Hammy too). Anyway, Mum no doubt will be doing her hobbies - cleaning the toilet, changing the sheets on big bed (I should think so too, can't beat fresh sheets) and ironing - so I shall make do with Dad for snuggle time. I can do snuggles with Mum tomorrow and Monday, that's unless Nanny turns up again on the prowl for food. Anyway ssssshh, dog sleeping.

I am in BIG trouble. I woke up on the sofa, but felt a bit queasy, so sloped down onto the rug, then it happened people. I did a little sickie burp, and hacked me up some bile - uuurrrgghh, it's left a vile taste in my mouth, and it didn't look very appealing on the rug… Ha ha Dad was shouting for Mum, "Oh Jesus H. Christ, Rupert's been sick", "Well fecking deal with it, FFS, what am I, the sick monitor?" Oh dear, I am in the bad books, well sorreeeeee, I couldn't help it, and besides it was probably that pebble shit, upset my sensitive tummy.

I remember once doing a full-on spewie, on a brand new wool rug. I had been on a walk and munched me a bit of grass, tasted sooooo good, and helps settle my stomach, anyway, we got back and in I trotted, only to get straight to the rug, and that's when I felt my insides turning out, HA HA, I was like exorcist dog, and it was all foamy and creamy and had bits of grass in it. I quickly tried to hide the evidence by eating the grass bit back up, but Mum caught me and was shouting very loud, "LEAVE IT!" - that made me jump, and so I was sick again, ha ha. The rug by the way was cream and grey, and I just so happened to get my aim right on the cream part. Mum was not happy, but to be fair, she didn't shout at me, as I put on my best sad dog eyes, and instead she comforted me.

Let's just say the rug was no more, and we now have tiled floors, mainly, and the rug in the lounge is beige, apparently hides sick well! Not that I am sick that often people, ok.

So, back to here and now, I am way over the biley vom episode and want me a treat, so I am going to see what Mum is up to and pester her…

Nom nom nom nommmmmm, this is the life, Mum has relented even though I have spewed and has given me this light tasting chicken thing, it's slim and a bit dried but tastes divine. I heard Mum say to Dad that they were all-natural and I could have the odd one - methinks the odd two or three would be a better number, but hey I have agreed to stick with the diet for a few more days. I need to tweet Clarice to see what her Saturday has been like, and also check on Stuffington and Mr Chicken, see if they are speaking.

OMG, I tweeted Clarice a pic of me with green slime coming out of my mouth, and added the caption "The Vominator", ha ha. She loved it, and tweeted back a funny line, "Vom be back!" Ooo she is funny, but hey NOT as funny as me, CAPICHE? I also tweeted Stuffington, well this is interesting… She has added Mr Chicken to her account, and it is now @StuffedChicken, ha ha ha. I am not sure about the name, but she said he has changed her life, and she is happier than she's ever been. I am pleased for them my BF has some company even if he is a stuffed bastard! Well it is evening, and I need to snuggle between Mum and Dad and watch me some TV, so if I don't come back, goodbye and goodnight… sssshhhh.

Sunday

I am staying in bed all day, snoozing and resting, no exercise for me OK? OH FFS WHAT?… Leave me alone will you, woman, NO NO NO… Ooooo food! I can smell something tasty, B.A.C.O.N.! You have got to be kidding me… I have to get my ninja skills honed and get down there double quick. Say a little prayer for me, people…

Well, you obviously didn't pray a) hard enough, b) loud enough or c) not at fecking all, you selfish rotten bastards! Yes it was bacon, yes Mum was cooking it, but NO I didn't get any, and neither did Mum, as she cooked it just for Dad, the greedy, hairy potato. Well he can piss off now, go on pack your bag, yes single bag, because that is all you will need, with your crap wardrobe. I am in a sulk, paw over face…

I have tweeted Clarice the injustice and a pic of me looking angry, I said I was going to teach them

a lesson. She came back and said, "Time goes on. So whatever you're going to do, do it, do it now". I am in awe of Clarice. I said I can't believe she loves my hero Robert De Niro as well. Of course, she said, he is amazing. Well that has made my Sunday, people, and cheered me up. Mum and Dad can go screw themselves today, I don't need them. Oh wait, I do, I have to go and relieve myself. Back soon.

Well, I reluctantly let Mum traitor-face take me for a walk, and we passed insane Douglas, I barked back today, I am that fed up with the charade. We also passed Ginger Bastard, he was doing his usual licking of his nut sack. I said, "do you do that to antagonise me, you bastard?" and do you know what he did - my god my eyes, my eyes! - the twat waved his nuts in my face, I have never been so insulted in all of my life! I will not be mentioning that again. We also passed Pomerbitch, haven't seen her for a while, still as yappy and high-pitched as ever. Wow broad, keep it down, yap yap yappy yap, yeah whatever.

We also briefly spotted what looked like another newbie, JEEZ get another estate to wander around, this is my patch! From what I could see though, he or she looked a bit on the rotund side, as I only caught the rear end and MY GOD, that ass was fatter than mine! I did attempt a run today - I looked like a little chubby cute wombat, just trundling along, ha. I am just so unique.

Back now, and have eaten the pebble shit, but as I was starving it tasted yummy. Now I have attempted some push-ups, I basically put my paws on the front of the sofa and pushed myself up. I did this three times, then Mum saw me and lifted me up, ha ha ha that was my plan all along. I feel like being waited on today, and as she has betrayed me, she can just be my slave for the day.

I am now in my favourite position of prostrate and snuggled next to Dad, who is obviously now leading a sedate life too, as he hasn't moved off the fecking sofa for two whole days. Mum is not impressed, but what do I care, if you feed him bacon this is what you get, payback. Now time for a nap. Oh wait, Mum is in the kitchen, I hope it's to make a roast beef dinner. OMG if I wake up to that, all will be forgiven.

Monday

When did it get to be Monday? My last thought was, Mum better be preparing a roast beef dinner, and save me some, and then nothing, blackness. OMG what if I have that "old timer's", along with my Arthur's ritus? I am finished people, the end is nigh. Oh wait, I do remember, Mum did NOT make beef, it was boring, something on toast, and so unimpressed was I that I slept and then I slept some more, so drama over. I suppose as it's Monday Nanny Hammy will be here, I shall just have me a scoot around first and then go and see. Ooo I'm scooting, I'm grunting, I'm surfing, people, whooo hooooo.

Well, I have made it downstairs. Dad went to work hours ago, and yes Nanny Hammy is here, and as per usual she is already filling her face… blimey, watch your fingers Nanny, she has just shoved a whole biscuit in her gob, Mum needs to have a word.

Ooooo, what is this I spy though, Nanny has left her handbag on the floor, and I can see something interesting sticking out. I need to investigate this further.

I am a ninja, I have gone and crept into the lounge and have stolen a glove from Nanny's handbag. It was fair game to be honest, as a) said handbag was left on the floor and b) the glove was just hanging out, there for the taking. I have run off with it, and when it gets a little warmer I'm gonna bury that bad boy in my patch. I am gonna tweet Clarice and BF and tell them about my trophy. They will be impressed.

I must remember to hide it in my comfy bed though, so I'm going to pretend I am having a nap and bury it underneath, ha ha, I am a genius! I wonder what else I can steal, this is so much fun. Oh Nanny is leaving, and so far so good, she hasn't noticed the missing glove. I just need to her to leave the house, then I am home and dry… She's gone! Now surely it must be time for a treat. I am starving, I am definitely under-nourished, I have been eating pebble shit now for five days and my shits are rock hard. I have even managed another run, well canter, ok trot, on my walk, and now I think it's the big weigh-in… Wish me luck, people.

YOU, people, are seriously going to have to all bow down to me - I am the KING, the CHAMP, the

MOST INCREDIBLE DAWG you ever did meet! I got weighed, and wait for it… wait…

Oh yes siree, I have lost a massive half a kilo, that is incredible! That's like two big shits of mine, or 2 apples, that's awesome! I have tweeted Clarice already, but she is snubbing me now, I think she is a little jealous. Stuffington on the other hand though was very supportive, and tweeted a pic of her and Mr Chicken in sports gear, aww you guys.

This is cause for celebration, so I think a treat is in order, don't you? I am off to show my best doe eyes… back soon.

Well that was a piss-poor reaction, as I got NIL, ZERO, NOTHING. I stood very patiently and didn't even whine, I just looked up at Mum and made my eyes into saucers, but she said, "No Rupert, you have done so well, who's a good boy?" Well what kind of a reward is that, "who's a good boy"? I can't eat that, can I, no I can't sit happily nom nomm nomming on them words, so if this is how it's going to be, I might have to scrap the diet. Yeah what is the point, you starve for a solid five days, and even throw in a few sit-ups and a run, for what, a "good boy"? Well you can piss off. I am tweeting Clarice.

Clarice was very understanding, and even said I should do my pretend collapse again to get sustenance. Great I am trying that.

It DID NOT work, Clarice you are an idiot. Mum has made an appointment now with the VET for tomorrow, as she said I could have a heart condition! Look what you have caused. I am freezing her out for an hour.

Tuesday

PISS OFF, don't even mention it, talk about it, discuss it or debate it, yes I have been to the vet's, NO I DO NOT have a heart condition, and YES I am still obese, ok? So go on, laugh all you like… The humiliation of being plonked on the scales again in an open area was disturbing. I mean why do they do that, for laughs, well do I amuse you? Am I funny to you? Well never again am I pulling that stunt, and as for Clarice, well she wants to be careful she don't end up in the patch HA.

I have already been on a walk, we went before the vet's, and as it was so goddam early, couldn't see shit out - well I could, me and my bionic eyes, but there wasn't a soul about. Came back and had half of the pebble shit, Mum said that was in case I had an accident.

I tweeted Clarice - I sent her a pic of me sitting next to a space hopper, and added the caption

"Spot the difference". She found it hilarious and retweeted it. I told her of my horror at the vet's, she apologised for suggesting the stunt, and I forgave her.

Sweary cat joined in today, I haven't heard from him in a while. He tweeted, "anyone tried to diet me, I would bite

their cocks off" - well that is a bit extreme, but very funny.

I noticed a tweet from Stuffington and Mr Chicken, she was positioned on his back and the caption was "Just playing Cluckaroo"! Ha Ha that is funny Stuffington, I retweeted it. I have a couple new followers, some uninteresting folk, oh wait, one has a pet cat called Bill, and he looks a bit flat-faced. WTF, I need to tweet and ask if he has been in an accident.

Ooops, well that was a faux pas, he hasn't been in an accident at all, and he called me a cheeky fat bastard! RUDE, when he doesn't know me. He said he was born that way and he was Persian, oooo very exotic! I did tweet an apology of sorts and thanked him for following me, although he may not now, but who cares, some people will never like me, and I will never give a flying …

So I need a snooze, all this activity this morning has seriously left me mentally exhausted, and as Dad as gone to work, it's just me and Mum. I will get to snuggle with her on the sofa, hopefully all day, so SSH.

What the hell, why, when I decide to go for a snooze, it is always disturbed by some racket or other? WHAT NOW? OMG, Mum is attempting some form of exercise, this I have to see… I shall be back…

I am wheezing, I don't even think I can speak right now, wait, just give me a minute… Oh jeez, all I can say is it's a good job Dad is at work, because if he witnessed what I just saw, he would have probably pissed himself, ha ha ha ha ha.

Mum was trying to follow some dance moves on the TV, and she has ZERO coordination anymore (she used to be a dancer/contortionist, so she says!).

Anyway, I stood behind her, mesmerised, wheezing and laughing, as the dance was, get this, HIP HOP! Well let me tell you, what Mum was doing was NOT hip hop - it looked more like hip popped, she looked like a crab on crack, and for the love of god, the music made no sense. I started barking, I had to warn her it was no good for her health, and she needed to stop this onslaught on my ears.

Thank god, she heard me, and stopped, but then no no no! she bent down and lifted me so I was just on my hind legs, and made me walk! GET OFF ME NOW, NEVER EVER make a dog walk on his hind legs, we are not performing monkeys or bears (although yes I do resemble a bear), BUT NO, PEOPLE, NO. I am not made for that shit - if I were, don't you think I would have been born with just TWO legs, you morons? I had no choice but to try and snap at Mum, which I do very, very rarely, but this occasion called for it.

I think she got the message, as she dropped my front paws, but then she said "Ow, naughty". I'M naughty, are you kidding me, you mad woman? I am going to my comfy bed, don't talk to me.

Thursday

Alright judging bastards, so what, I missed a day. Well firstly, I was still upset at being shouted at when I did nothing wrong, and secondly I needed my handsome sleep, also Twitter was crap, and so decided to lay off it.

So I have woken up in the big bed and Mum is still sleeping so I might have to wake her, but will be gentle - don't want to antagonise the woman do I?

I tapped her gently with my paw on the face, and then went in for a nose lick. "Aww is that my boy, come here then and give us a love." Yippeee, I forgive you Mum, now let's have a snuggle. In fact thinking about it, we could just do away with Dad in this big bed, think of all the room me and Mum would have, yes I might have to instigate a plan.

Well we are up and going for a walk, Mum says we are trying a different route today, thank god finally! Oh but it better be safe! No roads with fast cars I hope… Oh god, I hope she knows what she's doing, ppppfffftttttt, oops sorry I am little stressed but excited, I shall report back, pppfttt.

Well that was fun, whoooooo! We stayed on the estate (safe), but instead of turning right out of my gate, we turned left, and I was super excited at all the new smells. I had to stop at every single lamp post, brick wall, tree, bush, lawn, postbox and bin! and of course I left my wondrous scent on everything. We didn't see Douglas, thank god, but we did pass some newbies, and they all looked at me with such disdain, I could tell they were thinking who the f is he, and what is he doing on our patch. I didn't care, I was just glad of the peace and quiet.

That was, until we walked past a gate on the way back, and, from nowhere, the loudest, most frightening bark started! I actually cowered and stress farted again - pppfffttt, pppfftt - I was reminded of Folsom and the first night, that was it. I said NO, take me back, we are not coming this way again. I think I prefer Douglas thank you very much.

Back home and have eaten the pebble shit, kind of getting used to it now, I mean it does taste nice, at least it's not dry stick-to-the-roof-of-yourmouth crap! and it's healthy, yeah yeah, alright, I heard what I said… I am going for a morning snooze, DO NOT DISTURB.

What a snooze that was, but I am up and ready for action! I have done me a bit of yoga, stretched out and then did my usual downward facing dawg… I also attempted the slug, oh wait that's not a yoga position, sorry, that's one I made up. I actually crawl across the tiles like a slug, I love it as it's cool on my udders, it's especially nice in the summer. Now I need a treat - my sugars feel low - and I need to check Twitter.

I went to find Mum, but she was nowhere to be seen… I did panic a little at first, but then I realised the back door was ajar and she was out in the garden, so I thought to myself, oooo, opportunity, I can steal me another item to go with the glove for my patch! Yes that's right people, I still have Nanny Hammy's glove hidden in my comfy bed.

So off I went outside to have a mooch, and see what Mum was up to. Well she was sweeping up leaves, and I thought, that looks like fun, I will help, so I got right in amongst them and started throwing them up in the air. Mum was laughing, and took a pic of me - I will have to use that later for Twitter. I also started to bark at the giant brush thing, he is not as scary as black snake (arrrgghh!)… Well I soon got bored… I checked my patch, but the ground is still a little hard, so I went wandering into the shed.

I did think I better be careful, I don't want to get locked in like Ginger Bastard ha ha, so I barked to let Mum know. The shed was like Aladdin's cave, with all sorts of things tucked away in corners. I thought, what can I steal, and then I spotted it. There, lying on the floor, ready for the taking, was a stray golf ball. I thought what a result, that is some trophy for my patch, so I scooped it up in my mouth and bolted back inside (yes ok, "bolted" is a bit of an exaggeration).

Mum must have known I was up to mischief as I heard her shout, "RUPERT, what have you got?" Nothing! Must get it hidden quickly. I managed to get inside before Mum, and I deposited the ball under my comfy bed with the glove. I just had to hope and pray now that Mum wouldn't check.

Well she came in, and as I was sitting looking innocent in my bed, on top of said items, she just left me to it. YES! I cannot wait to tweet Clarice and BF to tell them.

I have tweeted Clarice and Stuffington, I sent my pic first of me in the leaves, adding the caption "Just Re-Leaving myself", ha ha. They liked it. I then tweeted my two finds for my serial killer patch, both were very interested in those. I checked the rest of my feed, a few from Sweary cat, ffing and blinding, and one from fat cat with a pic of her and some cream, yes you guessed it, the "cat who's got the cream".

I did get a treat people, so a happy little tail wag dance was in order, and although it was just half a grass stick (yes I know, I've been cut back), it was still nom nom nom.

I re-checked Twitter and there was a new tweet from BF Stuffington and Mr Chicken, they are going on vacation! WHAT!

Anyway, yes you have guessed it, I am going for a snooze in my bed to lie with my trophies until I get out hopefully next week and bury them, so goodbye for now.

Chapter 11 - Nothing

Diary,

Nope, got nothing. OMG I have writer's block, this is a catastrophe people, I am doomed! Ok, ok, stop with the dramatics, I hear you.

But on a serious note, I am staying away for the whole of the weekend, no diary, no Twitter, nothing, so amuse yourselves. I may be back Monday, I may not.

Stats

Treats: NOT A FAT LOT (ABUSE)

Birds stared at: Some

Pigeon Bastards Barked at: 2 twat bastards

and now

DOG BEING DOG

BYE.

Chapter 12 - The Great Camp Escape

Diary

Monday

What can I tell you? I am back and I have slept and slept and farted and slept some more, and, as promised, I stayed off Twitter for the whole of the weekend. Instead I actually played fetch Monkey Boy with Mum, it was fun, I forgot how much in fact, but I still don't really get the concept. Mum throws Monkey Boy, I then go fetch him, but then all I want to do is bite him and shake him, but no that's not the game, so I have to drop him at Mum's feet, and we start all over again. In fact this is probably why I get bored with it, invent something different will you? DUH… Anyway like I say I had a time out.

They are still feeding me pebble shit, but that might stop sometime soon, as I heard Mum say to Dad, "well I have weighed him again and he is the same". Well of course I am the same, idiot, I haven't morphed into a cat, have I? but apparently I haven't lost any more weight. I haven't the heart to tell her, I have been hiding my food, and Dad has been giving me his toast sometimes (sssshhh!). Ha ha ha, my plan will come to fruition very soon. I am a genius.

So anyway, I watched some David Attenborough last night, and it was my fave. They camped out for weeks to capture a scene where a huge crocodile leaps out the water and tries to grab a baby buffalo. I did some serious barking at the TV, Mum was egging me on, and at one point, I even managed to get on my hind legs and balance. I haven't done that for ages, so maybe I HAVE lost some weight and your scales are wrong, HA in your face.

Anyway talking of camping, I have to tell you people about the time Mum and Dad decided to embark on a weekend camping trip with me in tow, but before I do I just need to check Twitter and sniff out a treat… In fact it might be time to go back and check my serial killer patch, as it has warmed up slightly, and I can smell spring on the way. I am gonna mosey on outside and take my two trophies with me to bury.

Well I went and found Mum, and she let me out… I haven't quite managed to master opening doors myself, even though I am bionic dog. Outside, the air smells crisp and although it's cold, it's that fresh cold, it clears the old nostrils out. Off I went, straight to my patch, and I was like WTF? An intruder had been there, I could tell because a) the earth had been disturbed and b) there was a very musky, but enticing, smell.

I knew the smell, it was fox, and boy do I loves me a bit of foxy loxy scent all over my body, so I had no choice people, I had to roll and scoot around to cover as much of my body as I could with that lovely scent. It was only after about 10 minutes of rolling that I realised that the cheeky sly bastard had dug up my dental stick and it was gone, along with Socky, weird! Why he would want Socky god only knows. I was gutted at first, but did not worry for long as of course I have glove and golf ball to go in. I shall saunter back in to fetch them.

I've come back indoors to sneak my items back out, but wait, I can hear Mum shouting for me, so naturally thinking it's for a cheeky treat, I need to go and see. NO it's just Nanny Hammy here again, but oh wait she might have a treat for me, so "I'm coming!" ERM, WHAT? Why are you looking at me like that? Both her and Mum have an appalled look on their faces and are holding their hands over their noses. "Don't worry, I am not looking to stick my tongue up there, so what's the problem?" Huh, they are saying I smell disgusting. I BEG your pardon, I think I smell divine, like musk. What could be better than that?

Well, they strongly disagree, and obviously nothing smells quite like fox scent and so I had to be bathed. While Mum was lathering me up I heard Nanny shout, "Oh I meant to ask, you haven't seen a glove of mine, have you?" Well that was it people, I panicked, and I shot out of the bath, nearly fracturing my front legs! I had to get downstairs and quick. I heard Mum shouting after me, "RUPERT, you're still soaking wet!" I didn't care, I could not let Nanny find the glove, NO NO NO! I managed to get to the lounge in double quick time (must have been that ½ a kilo I lost), and plonked myself in comfy bed. Nanny Hammy thought I was escaping the bath and so tried to pick me up. I did a grumpy growl, she soon backed off. Then Mum came down and said, "what on earth is wrong with you?" I AM HIDING A GLOVE, IDIOT! Well, I was hauled back upstairs to get rinsed, and all the time I was thinking, you stay away from comfy bed, go and forage like you normally do.

Well my telepathy must have worked, because, when we came down, Nanny was sitting on the sofa, stuffing her face, what a shocker! and me, well I rubbed myself over every square inch of the house - rugs, sofa, bedding, everywhere - I just had to get MY scent back on me. Ha ha, drama over.

Checked Twitter, same freaks different day, well apart from my BF and Clarice. I tweeted her a pic of me in my patch and told her the drama, and about the foxy smell. She tweeted straight back and said she does the same, see MUM, the smell is divine. Anyway, Stuffington and Mr Chicken, weren't even active yet, probably still getting over their vacation!

Oh ok bye then Nanny Hammy, what, not enough chocolate biscuits for you to stick around for today? See you then… Right people now might be a good time to embark on the camping trip tale, buckle up people, it's a funny old story...

It was when I was younger, and a bit more boisterous, and less fat! Anyway, Mum and Dad thought it might be fun to go away for just a weekend at first, in a TENT, yes you heard right, and I was going with them and would be sleeping in said tent! Ha.

So Dad came home with all the gear, a tent, sleeping bags, blow-up air bed, barbecue, the works, and they also had a bowl for me! I ask you, selfish bastards… So all this stuff is piled high in the hall ready to be loaded in the car, and we were to set off early the next morning.

I was quite excited, but also a little anxious, as it was out of my comfort zone, but then I thought, oooo a journey to the countryside, fresh air, new smells, maybe get to see me some sheep and terrorise them… so anyway morning came and the day of the big adventure.

Dad loaded the car and put the big fluffy quilt on the back seat, the idea being that Mum would sit in the back with me and I would sleep most of the way. Let's just say sleep was not on my mind - I wanted to hang my head out of the window.

People, this next bit, it's uuurrghhhhhh, and WTF and OMG… We had been travelling about an hour and yes ok it was on bendy roads, but I didn't care, I was tongue-lolling out the window, but suddenly, the car stopped and Mum looked white and without any warning, projectile vomited over ME - uuurrgghhh - then over the quilt, over the back seat everywhere, and the smell, good god! I was hungry so tried licking it, not nice though people, not nice at all.

Dad got out and took me off Mum's lap, and started pouring bottled water over me, thank you Dad I thought… Mum was a mess, she got out of the car and spewed again all over the side of the road. I don't think Mum liked Dad's driving, as she was shouting at him, but he said well what the f***in' hell could he do about the roads? and it was her idea to go camping! Me, I was happy to relieve myself both ends and just have a good old mooch about.

They cleaned up her vom as best as they could and off we went again. This time Mum and me were sat up front with Dad, and we soon arrived at the campsite. People I was super excited - I could smell me some sheeps, ha ha ha this was going to be fun! But I wanted out of the car, it was a roasting hot day and I was irritable and thirsty. I needed to escape the vom-mobile, the smell was rancid. While Mum took the quilt to the local launderette, me and Dad did manly things, like relieved ourselves and drank beer, well Dad did, I just had water out of my bowl.

Once Mum returned, it was time for Dad to pitch the tent. It was seriously baking hot, so much so that Mum and I found shade under a large tree. Mum couldn't help as she had to hold onto me because the sheep in the next field were taunting me already. I was barking like mad, ha ha I loved it people, dumb bastards all bleat the same shit. Anyway after much exertion the tent was up.

Dad stood back, all proud and smug, but he looked very red and was dripping wet. Ooo, I thought, I shall run to him and lick him to congratulate him, and as I did I realised Mum hadn't quite got a hold of me, and before I knew it I was free and running… Even though my bungee was bouncing behind me, I did not care, people, I was FREE! I couldn't contain myself, and then suddenly I thought SHEEPS… I bypassed Dad and sprinted towards the field of bleating dreams.

OMG, I shot under the wire fence like greased lightning and before anyone could stop me, I was taunting them sheep good and proper. I ran rings round the thick bunch of blabbing bastards and started barking in their faces. They all started running in different directions and bleating, whooo hooo it was hilarious, ha ha.

However, people, this fun did not last long, as a) Mum came running and shouting so violently I thought she was going to murder me, and b) the owner of said sheep said if Mum didn't get me under control in the next 5 minutes he would shoot me, SHOOT ME, WTF? After I heard this I panicked and ran very fast towards another field, this was a BIG mistake people.

Unbeknownst to me in the very next field was a BULL, these bastards you do not want to mess with! Mum was puce, Dad was white, and I don't think I have ever seen him run with such speed, oh apart from that one time on the running machine… ha ha, memories.

Anyway, I finally had to stop to catch my breath and all of a sudden I felt me little legs being pulled from under me… I did think at first people my life had ended and I was leaving this world, but no Dad had scooped me up and was running full pelt out of the field.

After that I had to be staked to the ground, not literally people, don't panic! No, I had to stay on my lead, which was then secured to a massive metal pin in the ground. Spoilsports, I thought, I've never had so much fun, sheep shouldn't be so thick, and besides it wasn't like I was going to eat a whole one, come on.

Anyway, night-time fell, and I was exhausted from all the entertainment and it was time for getting inside the tent. Let me just say this folks, I WILL NEVER go camping again, e.v.e.r. Firstly the blow-up bed thing was horrendous - every time Mum or Dad rolled over, I was catapulted off it onto the floor, and then the sounds coming from outside the tent gave me the willies. Hoots and snuffles and farts (oh that was me, ha ha), but seriously it was pitch black, and yes I have bionic eyes, but inside the tent all I could see was tent FFS.

I couldn't wait for morning, and was so relieved when the sun came up I dive-bombed onto Mum and Dad. I think they were glad it was morning too, as Mum was moaning, and Dad was already packing stuff away… We didn't make the whole weekend people, we left that day, as Mum and Dad said it was a fecking disaster and couldn't risk me escaping again and then being shot. I was like fine by me, get me out of here, I don't want to be shot, no siree.

Dad drove back very, very fast and I had my head out the window, let me tell you I nearly lost my eyes, but I didn't care, it was heaven. We were going home, back to comfy big bed, and my toys… Never again people would we embark on such a treacherous expedition.

Oooo all this talk has made me very tired, I need to have a nap, and when I wake up I shall check Twitter and replenish my serial killer patch with my hidden trophies.

I couldn't nod off, I know, very unusual for me, but I am excited about getting out and burying my trophies. I shall just quickly check Twitter, no nothing of interest there, so I just need to alert Mum that I have to go outside. I shall do a whiny bark at the door, that often does it. Yes she is coming, I just need to mastermind my plan.

Right, I am mooching around outside, but Mum is still at the door… Piss off, just go back in, and leave the door ajar. I must have super powers because she has actually left the door open and disappeared. Now for "Operation Trophy Sneak". I have successfully managed to get back in without being seen and have scooped up the glove, I shall have to come back for the golf ball later.

Ha ha I am back outside with said glove, in your face Nanny Hammy! That's the last time you will see this baby, oh yeah. I'm digging, ooompf, nearly there, in you go glove, covering, kicking dirt over you, yes that should do it… ok, now for golf ball. OH, oh no no no, Mum is shouting for me… Oh jeez Louise she is coming to find me, quick I must hide.

"Rupert, Rupert, RUPERT, where the devil are you?" Well I am not going to tell you am I and give the game away? Sometimes Mum you are a dumb broad… Shit, shit, shit, she's found me, "what are doing in there, now look at you, I have just bathed you, for CHRIST SAKE, get in!" Alright, alright, calm down, wow. I shall have to bury golf bally another day - for now I need to get in!

Well, that has spoilt my fun, so only one thing left to do - go back to trying to have a snooze fest. See ya later…

Oh stats, I haven't given them for a while - Treats: one and a half (I know, miserly!)

Birds stared at: 5 (Yes they are back)

Pigeon bastards barked at: 1 (he was weirdlooking, brown and white!)

Tuesday

Hello people, YES AND… I am allowed to sleep through you know, I don't always have to report on what I did in an evening, but for your information, I tweeted Clarice about my escapade and checked on Stuffington and Mr Chicken, all is well. There was a tweet from the pig who I follow, eating a cupcake, mmmmmmmm cupcake… oh and I secretly chewed the golf ball, in fact it kept me occupied for quite some time, it was really hard. I nearly chewed my tongue off at one point, NO I didn't, really, what am I, retarded? DUH, but it now has some serious teeth marks in it, so it's hiding under comfy bed until I can get out there, hopefully today.

So that was last night, what did anyone else do? I bet the same, checked Twitter, and then vegetated in front of the TV… well that's what Mum and Dad did, looked like two potatoes, that's why you lot are called couch potatoes, I get it! I heard Mum say to Dad that she was thinking of just going back to giving me sausage pieces, as I was still as fat as a footstool. Dad laughed, I was like oi piss off, I am here you know, but then, YES, YES, YES, go back to sausage pieces, I telepathically shouted. I am sure it was transmitted - we shall see on Friday, when Dad has been shopping.

So Dad is at work obviously and Mum is somewhere, I think doing her hobbies again, so now could be a good time to get outside, but oh wait, I can hear her shouting for me, FFS is that all she does? "Rupert, Rupert, Rupert"… I am going to change my name and not tell her. OH Ok, coming. I need to go for a walk, so see you in a while.

Ha ha, that was interesting, just got back from my walk. We passed Frankfurter, he was sporting yet another new coat, some quilted country thing. I shouted that he looked like he had been bubblewrapped, he just smiled at me smugly. Then we passed Ginger Bastard, his collar was gone! I said, "oh how did you get that off without blowing your head up?" He said he very nearly strangled himself on the fence, so his Mum took it off. I said to him, "Christ you are a walking disaster, what with getting locked in sheds and now strangling yourself, you're a right old stunt cat." He liked that, said could I call him Ginger Bond from now on. I said ERM NO, he was more like Ginger Hardy, and not Tom! more like the one from the duo. Oh he was upset at that, ha ha.

We passed Douglas, but seriously I am bored with him now and his dumb ways, and then we passed Ian Beagle and Bassett, who I haven't seen for some time, I thought maybe he had died of sadness, but no, still the same sad eyes, god he looks miserable. I also spotted Shit Zoo guy, I really can't take to him, he is such a social snob. Well piss off mate, I didn't ask you to come on my patch, did I? Anyway the interesting part was the newbie that I briefly saw the HUGE rear end of was out and about, and it's a Bulldog. I was like WTF, how can you mix a bull with a dog? That's messing with nature, freaks, no wonder its arse was like the back end of a bus.

But to be fair, he was quite pleasant. His name is Henry and he has breathing problems, so sometimes has to stop and catch his breath, which may I add smells like rotten bins (I will not tell him this, noooo). So Henry is another newbie on the patch, I can't keep up with it all.

So back home and have eaten pebble shit as no sausage pieces have emerged yet, but I am not exercising anymore, and it doesn't look like Mum is either, so we can both just slob around. But first I just need to bury golf bally before Dad finds it, so I have to think of how I can get outside with it in my mouth… OH GOD, I am a genius! I will pretend I can see a mouse, and that will alert Mum and distract her at the same time. Ok, I am off to execute my plan.

Well, all hail Rupert, I told you I am a genius, a marvel and a mastermind! Not only did I get Mum to think there was a mouse, I also managed to slip past her in the doorway with golf bally in my mouth, HA HA.

I was crying loudly at the door, and scratching at it furiously, as I remembered the last time I did this, Mum came running. I started to bark even louder when she appeared and I pointed with my paw - HA HA NO I didn't, idiots - but I did do a little jump up on the glass, and smeared it good and proper with my saliva. Mum said, "What can you see, not another bloody mouse again I hope!" YES, I was shouting, a mouse, let me out to get him! I thought, any minute now she is going to open this door, so I quickly sneaked the golf bally out of comfy bed.

I absconded with him in my mouth, but now all I could do was a muffled whine, so I jumped up on the door again - seriously, I was knackered now, and thinking, just open the pissing door. Finally she opened the door, shouting "Go find him Rupert!" Well I totally forget I was supposed to be looking for a pretend mouse, and just ran to my patch. I had to act quickly, so I shuffled dirt with my paws, and buried golf bally in a haphazard fashion, it would have to do.

I then barked a little and ran to the shed, and Mum thought the mouse had run under it, so I barked some more and sniffed back and forth a little, just to make it seem I was hunting the pretend bastard out. It worked because Mum shouted, "OK Rupert, come on boy, I think you scared him off, time for a treat!" OH YEAH BABY, what did she say, treat? OMG if I had known pretend mouse would win me a treat, I would've done this ages ago.

Nom nommmm nommmmm nomm nomm, I am in a dental stick haze people, don't talk to me, I am savouring this moment, mmm bliss.

Well, that was nomlicious, yes it's a word, I've checked my doggie dictionary… Ok, I know I sometimes get confused with certain words, but that is real. So I have checked Twitter and I cannot believe that Stuffington and Mr Chicken are trending, WTF?

This is outrageous! They have taken a pic of them both together with the backdrop of New York and hash tagged it #Stuffyinthecity. OMG how the hell has this happened, and why am I NOT trending? I am a comedy genius! Right, this calls for action, I need to think of something, and I NEED to trend, people, it's my birth right, give me a minute will you, oh god the pressure… Ok I've got it.

If THAT doesn't trend, then I shall eat my own tail, well I would if I could catch that bastard, always just one step ahead, every goddam time! So anyway, I have put a pic on of me and made myself enormous (yeah alright, I hear the laughs) and I am standing over the Empire State Building and I hash tagged it #Dogzilla. I bet if you measured my IQ it would be like 200 or more I am that clever. I shall see later if I trend, then I can be as popular as my BF Stuffy.

Well what a day, I think I need to have me a welldeserved snooze, so I am off for a nap… only wake me for treats.

ZZZZZZ ZZZZ ZZZZZZ

WHAT, Christ almighty, Dad is home and he has somehow crept in, changed into his "lounge wear" (yeah right I mean pyjamas!) and he is now prostrate on the sofa. I better not have missed my evening meal, I will protest fart otherwise… In fact I am going to find Mum, I believe she is in her favourite room of the house, the kitchen, yes I shall mosey on through.

Well, I finally made it to the kitchen and yes Mum was there, cooking their evening meal. I was like, "WHOA, where is Rupert's? can you not see I have wasted away? gimme, gimme my food!" I should think so too, you were very lucky there Mum.

I was moments away from dropping the atomic bomb of farts on you, so lucky escape. Well I can waddle back to the lounge now, Mum is bringing me my evening snack, although I think it is still pebble shit, but food's food… Back later.

I am going to keep this brief: I have eaten, I have relieved myself, and now I am snuggled between Mum and Dad on the sofa to watch an episode of Game of Thrones, and as it's been a while since I last saw it, I want complete silence, so piss off, do not disturb and I shall see you in the morning. Goodnight.

Friday

I suppose you want to know what happened to Wednesday and Thursday, well here's what happened, I was enthralled with Game of Thrones Tuesday night and stayed up extra late, like until 11 p.m., and then I slept in until 11 a.m. Whooo hoooo! that was an amazing snooze fest.

I then had time out because I DID NOT trend. Yes you heard, I don't understand it either. I mean how the hell can my BF and a stuffed chicken get more attention than me, a genius dog? It is a catastrophe and so I took to my bed to sulk. But then I remembered my patch and that golf bally was only half hidden, so I went out and covered him good and proper, then had me a mooch about, and guess what I came across, can you guess? NO? Well I shall enlighten you, I came across a DEAD mouse, yes that is right people, D.E.A.D., and it was not killed by me.

It looked sad, and this made me sad. I think it was Ginger Bastard who killed it and left it there for me as a trap, after the other morning, when I barked at him and said he was more like Hardy… well payback is a bitch, and I shall get my revenge. I obviously had to inform Mum about dead mousey, she was in fact sad too, even though she wouldn't want one as a pet in the house! So we buried him, but NOT IN MY PATCH thank god, don't want that decaying filthy rotten rodent round my stuff.

So that's what happened for two days, and now it is Friday and Dad has gone shopping, and Mum and

I are tidying. Yes I am helping, I have grabbed my blanket off the sofa and I am rolling around in it on the floor, this should clean the rug… Oh no no no no, I hear the den door being opened, holy crap, black snake is coming out! Quick let's run and hide, shit, shit, shit, I am stuck under the blanket, it's tangled around me… Oh god I can't breathe, I am going to die and black snake is going to suck me up, HELP, EMERGENCY, CALL SOMEONE! Ppppfffttt, oh great that is all I need, ppffft, CRAAAAPPPPP, get me out, Mum, Mum, Mum, Mummmeeeeee! Oh thank god she is coming… "Rupert, you daft sod, why have you wrapped yourself up in the blanket?" ERM, are you thick? I haven't, you gormless broad, I am trapped, can't you see? JEEZ, just let me out.

I'm FREEEEE, ha ha! Oh wait, what is she doing now, oi get out of my comfy bed, what is she saying - "Rupert, you haven't seen a glove of Nanny's have you, or know where it is?" Errrrmmm yes I know where Nanny's glove is, I also believe you know where the treats are, but if you think I am going to tell you, well two words, PISS and OFF, ha ha. You will never find glovey again, now give me a treat or else.

Well that threat worked, NOT, and I am upstairs, out of the way of black snake. I can hear him taunting me, with the ridiculous vvvvrrrooooommm sound he makes, tosser! I wish she would hurry up and put him away, I want Dad back with the shopping, and SAUSAGE PIECES. Ooooo I hear silence, oh and the door, Dad is here! I am coming, I'll just scoot myself around a bit first, oh yeah, ooo god that feels marvellous, scoot, scoot, scooting… right, I am off, I spy with my bionic eye something beginning with S.

SAUSAGE PIECES are back people, and I am in seventh sausage heaven, so you got it, can't talk, nom nom nommmmmmmmm, back later.

I have made Mum promise never to change me from sausage pieces again. How did I do this I hear you say, well I basically pointed with my paw to the sausage pieces bag, and barked. Ha ha ha don't be so ludicrous, I haven't made her promise, but I have made a point of turning my nose up at the pebble shit, so she will get the message.

Oh I forget to say I went for a walk this morning, and yes I spotted Henry, he was struggling with his breath, but I didn't get too close, I wasn't in the mood for rotten bins! I did shout hi and he saluted me. I saw Frankfurter and Pomerbitch, and then I spotted Ginger Bastard. I shouted, "Oi, a word, you dirty traitor you"; he hissed and tried to take a swipe but my ninja kung fu skills came in handy and I dodged his paw. I said to him, "was it you who left me a present in MY garden?" He feigned ignorance and said he knew nothing of any mouse. "HA", I said, "I did not say what it was, so it WAS you! Well ginger shit bastard, I have left my shed door open, and it has a trip wire on it, so STAY OUT OF MY GARDEN, you filthy shit bag bastard!" He soon backed off, and slunk away with his tail swishing. I was pumped and trotted back, yes trotted! with Mum, ready for the day.

So have been on Twitter, still not trending… Tweeted Clarice and told her, she said she would retweet it, and anyway I would always be on trend with her. Maybe we should tweet a pic together and hashtag that, how about #fatbottomeddawgs? She likes it, it's tweeted. Hmm, no more new followers for a while, I must be losing my edge… I shall tweet a joke a two, that always gets a laugh.

Tweeted this instead:

"Official Dog Song

Every snack you take, every food you make,

every can you shake, every seal you break,

I'll be watching you…"

Ha ha, already it has had over 40 likes. I am BACK! Yeah baby, I can feel the big time is upon me, and soon EVERYONE WILL KNOW MY NAME, and will be chanting it - "Rupert, Rupert, Rupert" - but for now, snooze time. Sssshhhh, sleeping.

Oh stats

Treats: 2

Birds stared at: several, all at once; I went crosseyed!

Pigeon bastards barked at: 3, RODENT WINGED BASTARDS

Saturday

It's the weekend, it's the weekend, I'm gonna spend ma money! though technically I don't have an allowance or any money, only dog biscuits, and they are not accepted as valid currency, what gives? So people yes it's Saturday, and that means Mum and Dad are here all day, and I think Nanny Hammy and Granddad potato are coming round later, yes for food, again. Their pantry must be bare, or they are creating a massive stockpile of food in case the end of the world is nigh.

So for now, a walk is in order and a check of Twitter, oh and sausage pieces, nom. I have been on my walk and I have nothing to report, well other than we spotted the Pugly Club. Mum shouted the diet was off, I swear he sniggered, PISS OFF mate, at least I am still handsome, PAH! Back home now and Dad is in the garden, so I have to go and do manly things with him. Back later. If you want, go and check on my Mum, but she is doing hobbies again. She loves that toilet-cleaning hobby of hers.

OOOOOOOO it was very exciting - Dad is preparing the greenhouse again for this year's crop. I am helping, I am a good boy… "FFS Rupert, get out of the way!" Erm excuse me, I was only trying to help tip the soil out like you wanted! No respect… I ask you, I have giant paws, I can dig, I was putting it on the greenhouse floor for you… Jeez, I am going to check my patch, also see what I can find to bury.

YES, the shed is open and I have found me a dried up ball of worms, wowzers, this is awesome! Uurrgh it doesn't taste very nice and it is a bit stringy… oh well, I can bury it, come on wormy ball to your new home, never to be seen again… what? Dad is shouting to Mum - hang on…

"Have you seen that garden string, I left it in the shed" "No, are you sure you put it in the shed?" "FFS YES!"

Oh I have no idea what they are going on about, it doesn't concern me, so I am just going to waddle to my patch… NOOOO, must hide quick, Dad has spotted me… he is running over to me… This is mine! Finders keepers, right? No no no, mine mine mine, gerroff, no YOU lose it… "RUPERT, drop it!" NO, ggggrrrrr… "Drop it NOW!" Oh here then, if it means so much to you, have it, why would I want a wormy ball anyway.

Oh what's that, you're shouting to Mum that you have found the string - "well probably right in front of your eyes, as per usual", I always hear Mum say that to you, that you can't see further than your nose. Not like me, I have bionic eyes, blind bastard. Oh well that has spoilt my fun, suppose I had better go and check on Mum, see if I can get me a treat, and then wait for Nanny and Granddad.

Stretching, ooooo let me see if I can reach the end of the rug, whilst still hanging half out of my bed… maybe I could see if I could drag my bed with me, I am going to try, ooomppf this is harder than I thought! I've abandoned the idea, my comfy bed looks nice in the middle of the room. "Rupert have you moved your bed here?" NO don't be such an idiot, why would I do that? god, so stupid sometimes, anyway I hear Nanny and Granddad… going to get me a kiss and a treat.

Whoo hooo, Nanny Hammy has given me something yummy, it was a chocolate-coated (don't panic DOG CHOCOLATE ok), bone-shaped biscuit, and it was lip-smacking lovely! I want another one, pleading eyes are in order… Oh hang on, what is happening, I can hear movement, humping? Dad is wet, OMG are they are having an anniversary, that is totally disgusting with Nanny Hammy and Granddad here, FFS you humans do the weirdest shit. I need HELP, CALL
THE NUMBER! Oh hang on, no, no, I could be wrong, Mum is in the lounge with Nanny, OMG that is worse, what are you doing with Granddad? WHOA, why are you moving BIG BED, what is happening?? Pppfffttt, pppfffttt, pppfffttt, OH GOD anal gland expulsion alert.

"Rupert, it's ok boy, Mum and Dad are not moving, or leaving"… Well I am not really bothered about Dad leaving, but I am concerned with where my BIG BED is going - where am I going to sleep? "We are having a new bed delivered, Granddad is helping move the old one out."

Oh thank Christ on a bike for that, ooo a new big bed! Oh hang on - Dad is limping, Granddad and Mum are laughing (sadists!). I must go to him, "I am here Dad, what's happened, I am not laughing!" "Rupert, get out from under my feet!" Well charming, piss off then. I hope your foot drops off, bastard twat, wasn't my fault you stubbed your fat toe, should have had shoes on instead of those hideous ridiculous Philip flops you wear all the time.

So that's why Nanny and Granddad are here, but suppose they are stopping for lunch, eating us out of house and home again… oh here we go, Nanny is already on the biscuits, all right Nanny, easy there, the trough's that way! Oh I am fed up with this drama - going to check Twitter and tweet Clarice and BF about new big bed.

Clarice said that she has to sleep on a bed at the end of big bed because she can't get up on it. I said well your Mum should lift you up, but she said that wouldn't help as she likes to wander at night, looking for snacks. Ha ha, I like Clarice and her way of thinking. Stuffy said she wished she had a bed, so I should consider myself very lucky, she sleeps in the pantry.

Well, Nanny and Granddad have finally left and we are just waiting now for new big bed… hang on, wait I can hear a delivery vehicle, I know the sound well, what with him next door. I shall bark and alert everyone, "BIG BED IS HERE, BIG BED EVERYONE!" Quick get the door, what, why can't I come out and help? I can supervise… No? Oh ok then suit yourself.

I am locked in the den with black snake, I DO NOT like this one bit, thankfully I have bitten him before he could get in first and it has done the trick, he hasn't made a peep, ha! I can hear movement and more humping… Oh wait, Mum is shouting for me, YEAH well unless you think I have grown five foot tall and have thumbs now, you better come and open the door! Honestly, she would not qualify for Mensa.

OMG, words cannot describe the soft, luxurious, most amazing feel of the new big bed! It is very very bouncy and I have had so much fun already… Mum let me wriggle all over it and I side scooted, back scooted, front scooted, and even rolled over several times until I was dizzy. I cannot wait for night, night time, this has turned out to be the best day ever.

And guess what people, Clarice and I have trended, yes that is right, you heard, the hashtag #fatbottomeddawgs was a hit. I am going to be a star.

Well I need to have a snooze, so catch up with you later… bye for now.

Stats

Bleurgh I can't be bothered.

Sunday

I AM NEVER GETTING OUT OF THIS BED, ever! That was the best sleep I have had for a long time. This new big bed is incredible, for starters it is much bigger, so I have even more room to stretch my legs out. I tried touching Mum's back with my paws, I couldn't reach, and the comfort on my Arthur's ritus, well my joints feel young again. I might bounce, yes I am going to try it, whoo this is so much fun, I am bouncing my front paws up and down into the soft mattress… "Rupert STOP IT!" Oh piss off, why do you always spoil my fun? Well nose lick time, come here, who's first, whose breath isn't as dragon-like?

It was Mum, as her breath wasn't as rancid as Dad's, I think he ate rotten dead mousey before he went to bed, or he kissed Henry, yuk. Anyway I have finally relented and got up out of big bed and now downstairs, and as it is Sunday, it's snooze day.

Well I have snoozed most of the day away, not even checked Twitter really… I think the big bed has relaxed me, and it is now evening, not much happening. I am counting the hours before I can get back upstairs to heaven. Dad was his usual prostrate self on the sofa, farting, uurrgh disgusting.

Mum was busy with her hobbies, and now both are on the sofa, I shall go and squeeze between them and see if there is any David Attenborough. I shall check back later.

Chapter 13 - The End is Nigh

Diary

Monday,

I slept solid again, this new big bed is awesome. I watched some David Attenborough last night, another favourite, one where these monkeys have to live in a sparse desert on cactus. I had me a right good bark at them, they reminded me of my Monkey Boy.

Anyway Mum has woken me today with lots of kisses and hugs… Something is off, it better not be a trip to the vet's, I will feign paralysis… I am not going to that god awful place, I am getting out of her grip, ooompf, I'm free! (ooh sound like camp bastard shit zoo! HA) Now just need to get off the bed, wheeeeee, I've jumped and am now bunny-hopping down the stairs.

Dad must have gone to work, and I bet Nanny Hammy will be here any time, but for now I have the lounge to myself until Mum comes down, so while I wait I just might do me a little breakdance bottom shuffle… whey hey I am spinning round and round, this is ace! "RUPERT, stop that!" Oh bollocks I didn't hear Mum come in, is she a ninja or what? "I hope you haven't got worms, come here let me see…" NOOOOOOOO, I must escape, I do not have worms, woman, I was just dancing, now gerroff.

I am going to check Twitter, relay my fears to Stuffy and see what she reckons… well I have tweeted my BF, and said Mum was being super loving this morning, and my spidery senses are on high alert. She tweeted back a pic of herself as a tarot reader with the caption "I see doom and gloom, I see an empty bowl, I see neglect". Oh piss off, some use she was, and if that prediction is true, well I am going to freeze Mum out, I will just give all my attention to Dad, let's see who cracks first!

Oh goody, the door! Nanny Hammy is here, she will save me, and hopefully have a treat for me… waddle, waddle, waddle, I'm coming Nanny… "Where's my Rupert, come here and give Nanny a big kiss!" Erm, WHAT, this is seriously odd… Nanny does sometimes let me kiss her, but only when I force myself on her. I like to feel her chin hair on my face - it tickles - but I don't usually get asked to kiss her voluntarily. Something is happening!

Well, I am lying in my comfy bed, I am seriously stressed, ppppffftt, told you! Nanny and Mum are sitting talking on the sofa, so far I have picked out the word "neglect", yes that's me, abandoned, me again! and "we can't just leave her there". Leave who, where? Who is HER, what are they going on about? Well for once I wish Dad would come home and shed some light, and save me from this weird talk. OMG maybe Stuffy was right in her prediction!

Oh, we are going for a walk, I hope to the park with the squirrel bastards, yes that would help me, please, please please let it be squirrelly park.

It wasn't pissing squirrelly park, it was duck bastards, and even they couldn't shake my ill feeling. All round the park I kept hearing odd phrases, like "well he will adjust", "he won't be lonely any more", "he will get more exercise"… HA that's it - maybe Dad has a new fitness regime! I can stop worrying now and get in amongst these duck bastards. Come here you quacking idiots...woof, woof, woof, woof!

Well Nanny Hammy has gone and Dad's back and I can hear Mum saying to him, "well we need to call and make an appointment first, then we can take him along to see her". Again who is this "her"? See who? I can see perfectly fine thank you. Weirdos talking in riddles! I am going on Twitter.

I have tweeted a pic of me mid-bark with a duck in the background, caption "just ducking! and diving today". HA HA, that has got quite a few likes already. People are suckers for an animal pic, everyone is social media mad these days, god knows how you humans communicated back in the day… What did you do, send a pigeon round Bob's or sommat, "hey Bob, did you hear about Dave? he's got piles" and Bob sends back, "piles of what?" HA HA you are all backward dummies , we are so superior to you, admit it, now bow to me.

I need a nap, so I am off to see if I can snuggle next to Mum on the sofa... yes she's there, see ya later... big zzzzzzs is what it's all about.

I've woken up to the sound of Mum and Dad talking in code again, and they are on about us all going for a drive tomorrow, so Dad can't be going to work… I told you this was odd, but maybe we are going to the country and camping again, oh boy that was fun, do you remember, people? Ha ha ha… I wish they would tell me, this is stressing me out, ppppffffftttt, oops sorry. I need a snack, so off I go foraging.

I briefly checked Twitter, few more likes to my pic and one more new follower, a random soul, obviously looking to jump on my popularity bandwagon! Well let me give them some fodder to retweet… I have just tweeted myself doing my breakdance move from this morning, caption "Just doing the hot bum shuffle". That should send them into a frenzy!

Well, I have had a snack, it was a very uninteresting bone- shaped biscuit thing, but it tasted of salmon, YUK, I don't want that again. I may have to go for another snooze, as today has been quite stressful for me, and my Arthur's ritus is acting up from the romp around the park, so wake me Diary if anything occurs.

Tuesday

Goddam, it's a) Tuesday, I know, I know, and b) early, like 5 a.m. or something ridiculous and c) both of them are still sleeping, and I am crammed down the bottom of the bed. How did this happen, and why I am at the bottom of the bed? OMG, we are going somewhere today as well, now I remember, maybe it is a massive surprise and it's a brand new park! I hope so… I am going to try and wake Dad this morning, I just hope his mouth is closed, otherwise, phew weeeeee… Thank God it's closed, but he is lying on his side, I need to try and get over him, oooommmppppfffffff! I am on his head, if this doesn't wake him nothing will… Ha ha, he can't see, my udders are in his eyes. "Get off me Rupert, you big lump of lard!"

How very rude and hurtful! Well screw you, Mum will love me… Tapping, poking, oh yeah, Mum is up, I win again. Ha ha, I love this game. Come on, let's go and see what bastards are out this morning.

The walk was totally boring, it was dark and so early we passed not another soul, so I am back now people, and I have even eaten my breakfast, which was quite tasty. Mum and Dad are dressed, and he is whispering again. What IS IT?! Oh ok we are going out to the car, no special blanket, interesting… I shall report back later people.

OMG, like WTF, like seriously! Like OMG, OMG, we went to what I thought looked like a farm, and at first I thought, oh ok, let's look at some pigs and cows, we can compare udders.. But no, when we get to the end of the driveway, it looks like Folsom Prison, so my anal glands started up and my farts, good god, it was like Hiroshima all over again! I had terrible flashbacks, the horrors. I thought, you better not be leaving me again, I will run away for sure.

But no, some butch woman came out and she was holding this dog, and I thought, how odd, can't it walk? oh what a shame, but then Mum and Dad went up to the dog and started petting her, and then took her off the woman… I was like, this day is just getting weirder and weirder. Then they put her on the floor, and she could actually walk, in fact she started trotting round me and sniffing. I tucked my tail under and thought, you can piss off… she then whispered in my ear, and said, "I am going to be your new sister!" WHOA!!! Hang on there, tiny! WTF, NO never, not on your nelly, what kind of mental insane talk is this? As De Niro would say, "what are you, stupid?"

I started looking up at Mum and Dad, but they were talking to the butch woman, and saying, "well, we will come back at the weekend" and "yes we will leave a donation". WTF? If they think they are donating me, they can piss off. I am planning my escape.

Well, thank god, we are leaving, and that mad cow is still there, phew! I do not know what kind of nonsense she was spouting, but you ain't coming to my house. Bye bye.

Saturday

Well people, that is it, kill me now, you are not going to believe it, Mum and Dad have only gone and got a rescue dog to keep me company. WTF!! It's a she, and it's a Jack Russell, but she is not fat like me. However, she is old, and she is soooooo yappy, she barks at everything, from a leaf outside (dumb broad) to the postman, and MY god

she does not like him.

I knew something was off the other day, when they took me to Folsom Prison! I thought, Holy Christ, they are going to leave me, selfish, selfish bastards, but no, they just had a wander around, and we saw that yappy little cow, who started sniffing my bottom (thank the lord it was clean)… I thought, gerroff, what are you doing mad bitch? and then she started saying she was going to be coming home with me. I was incensed, let me tell you, I told that broad, no way Jose, you can piss right off.

Well, we left without her, and I was like all laughing and stuff, and in fact she was still on the driveway as we went by, so I gave her the paws up sign, and shouted HA in your face bitch! Of course she started yapping, and even bared her teeth! Phew, I was glad I was in the car.

But, people, it all blew up in my face, and a few hours later, I was left on my own, which was very weird. The last time I got left completely on my own was when Mum had to take Dad to the hospital, she thought he was having a heart attack. In fact it was worse, he had a kidney stone or something, and had to wait to wee it out. He was in a lot of pain, and I remember the day it actually came out of his winkie, because he started shouting, "it's out, it's out!" I went running expecting to see a giant rock, well people, it confirmed it, my Dad is a huge pussy - this thing was no bigger than a grain of rice, I was like, what was all the fuss about? Anyhow, being left was strange, and I just wandered from room to room, shouting, "hello, it's me!" So this time round I knew what to expect, but it was still weird. All I could do was wait.

It did not take long, and, as soon as the front door was opened, I stretched myself out yoga style. I thought, I am not going to give them the benefit of thinking I was lonely, I shall make out I was snoozing (I was in fact in my comfy bed with Monkey Boy HA), but they can piss off. Just as I was about to waddle to the door, BAM, I was nearly knocked sideways - that's when I heard it, yapp, yapp, yapp, yapp. My heart sank, and I thought, you have got to be kidding me, NOOOOOO, that's

But it's real, people, as real as my farts. They brought the rescue broad home, and I suppose you want to know her name. It's Titch (the Bitch, Ha), and she does not shut up from morning till night… It's only been seven days, and yes she already sleeps in the big bed with Mum and Dad. How is this possible, I hear you say, well trust me I don't pissing know, but it is possible, and she gets to lie next to MY MUM, arrrggghh! Until we go to bed, she is constantly yapping for something, and she has an obsession (worse than my football one) with a tennis ball, she carries it everywhere, and if it goes missing, god help you, she whines and cries and circles until it's found. She is defective and I wish they would return her, but that is not the worst, nooooo no no - she likes to wind me up - daily, hourly, in fact every goddam second.

She gets right up in my face, turns round and then twerks. WTF, she knows I am impotent and cannot be that way anymore. I did in fact try and hump her on the second day, it was a disaster. Picture a fat old giant tortoise trying to get on his mate, then having the misfortune to not make it and roll over, that was me… I couldn't quite get up high enough and my udders got in the way, then she turned sharply and bit me on my neck, and I ended up rolling on my back like a beached whale, it was not attractive. Then she laughed in my face, said served me right for giving her the paw at the kennel! So I suppose we are equal, but this torture I endure every day is hell.

Day four with Mad Bitch (that's what I'm calling her), the postman came with a parcel, probably for him next door again… Now me, I am not fussed about him personally, that's the postman. (Him next door does my goddam head in, all his shit he orders…) Anyway this crazy mutt, OMG, she went nuts, started yapping, head shaking, running from room to room, even jumped up on the chair close to the window and shook all the scatter cushions over the floor. Mum was not happy… I saw this as an opportunity to get in there and say see, she's broken, send her back, but to no avail. I think Mum knew she was defective and that is why they have taken her in, which is kind I suppose, but Jesus, she's more disturbed than Douglas… Talking of whom, we passed him together yesterday morning, and he was somewhat confused - he started his bark, bark, bark, but then Mad Bitch started to yap back and she even raised her hackles. I was like, whooaa, it's only Douglas, back off, but she whispered to me that Douglas was an imposter! I said, "don't be such an imbecile, FFS, what is he disguised as, a giant mouse? ha ha… You need to get your eyes tested". So she bit me.

We spotted Henry, and she was very rude to him and shouted, "urrrghhh, your breath stinks mate, ask your Dad for a minty stick!" I was like totally embarrassed and said, you cannot go around telling other dawgies they smell". She bit me again.

What is even more gross and disgusting is, she eats poo, yes you heard me people, she eats SHIT. I said, "you wanna go and live with Ginger Bastard, you would fit right in with him, as he shits in his house, think of the feast, OMG, WTF, why do you eat shit?" She said it was a bad habit she had gotten into, and it was not a story for now, as it brought up terrible memories of the time she was abandoned and had no food.

Oh my god people, even I have a lump in my throat… I said, "well it's a habit you are going to have to break, I am not sleeping next to a shitbreathed individual, CAPICHE? and besides you will NEVER go hungry here, well I say never, it depends on if I have had my fill, and if you walk away from your bowl, it's fair game ok". She said she would try.

However, my life is now officially ruined, Mad Bitch even wants me to add her to my Twitter account! I have stood my ground on this one though and said get your own, you are not feeding off my fame.

Talking of Twitter, I have checked my account and reported this disastrous fiasco, and now my BF and Clarice

want to see a pic of her, so reluctantly I have posted us sitting together, seemingly happy (not). Stuffington loves her already. Clarice said, is there any room in my patch? Ha good one, I said, my day surely could not get any worse…

NOOOOOOOO, no no no, I am going to have to think of ways to get rid of this mad bitch! When I got to my bed, guess who was in it? Yes, her. I am depressed beyond belief, I am going to bury that bitch in my patch… "I have to think about that one shot, one shot is all it is gonna take… That mad bitch has to be taken with one shot." Then I get my life back and all is restored to harmony.

OOO, I hear Mum calling! Must be time for either my breakfast or walkies… see you later…

That was interesting, it was for breakfast, and Mad Bitch turned her nose up at hers, so of course, I was like, waste not want not - I got straight in there and wolfed it down. If this continues, she can stay, as extra portions for me sounds divine. Only trouble is, now I am so laden with food, I really do need a nap, but I can hear my lead so have to try and muster the energy for a short trundle out… Let's see who is out and about today.

Ha, ha, ha, I don't think Mad Bitch has seen a cat before, weirdo! As we passed Ginger Bastard on the walk, she went proper mental, I thought she was going to break her bungee, Mum couldn't even get control of her. I was laughing so much, it caused one of my asthmatic wheezing fits. Mum was then concerned for me and as she bent down to calm me, all hell broke loose - Ginger Bastard actually had the nerve to come right up to Mad Bitch and swiped at her with his stinking ginger paw and it caught her on the nose, she was yelping and yapping like she had been punched by Mike Tyson! I shouted, "calm down Titch" (I thought I better use her actual name, or it would only make the situation worse)… She did in fact stop yapping, must have been the shock! so I waddled up to her, and on the way growled at Ginger Bastard and said, "do one, pussy, or there's a shed I know of just waiting for a cat like you", HA. I then found myself comforting Titch, something I thought I would

never do, but decided that if she is here to stay, and it looks that way, may as well have her as my companion and on my side, rather than the furenemy!

And so, people, we have called a truce, and Titch and I are now friends, and do everything together. She told me the reason she is so crazy is that her previous owners used to leave her for hours and

hours, and then when they did come back, they would just ignore her, so to try and gain attention she would yap, but this made them angry, until one day, they dumped her at the concrete jungle place, which scared her half to death.

So I have told her she never has to worry again and she will be loved and kept safe always here with Mum and Dad and me, and I even let her join my Twitter account and changed it to @RupertTitch, so check us out and come follow us, especially if you liked my diary. Also Titch does have a voice, like I say a very yappy constant one, but if you want to hear what she has to say, then you will need to wait for her journal, which is called "My Journey - Titch's Tail"! That is all for now Diary, thanks for listening.

The End

Acknowledgements

I would like to thank my PA… erm yes I have one! Ha… jealous much? She is the lovely Cathy Morton @CathyLaQuinta… Without her kindness, generosity and skills, this book would still be gathering dust.

A big thank you to my Mummee, Dad, Nanny Hammy and Granddad potato for letting me insult you.

36429316R00141

Printed in Poland
by Amazon Fulfillment
Poland Sp. z o.o., Wrocław